THE
SMALLER
EVIL

STEPHANIE KUEHN

THE
SMALLER
EVIL

DUTTON BOOKS

Dutton Books
An imprint of Penguin Random House LLC
375 Hudson Street
New York, NY 10014

Copyright © 2016 by Stephanie Kuehn

This is a work of fiction. Names, characters, places, and incidents either are the product of the author's imagination or are used fictitiously, and any resemblance to actual persons, living or dead, businesses, companies, events, or locales is entirely coincidental.

Printed in the United States of America

Library of Congress Cataloging-in-Publication Data

Names: Kuehn, Stephanie, author.
Title: The smaller evil / Stephanie Kuehn.
Description: New York, NY : Dutton Books, [2016] | Summary: "Chronically sick and anxiety plagued Arman Dukoff runs away to attend a self-actualization retreat where he eventually discovers both a bloody corpse and a sense of self that was not what he bargained for"—Provided by publisher.
Identifiers: LCCN 2015035869 | ISBN 9781101994702 (hardback)
Subjects: | CYAC: Self-actualization—Fiction. | Anxiety—Fiction. | Coming of age—Fiction. | BISAC: JUVENILE FICTION / Social Issues / Depression & Mental Illness. | JUVENILE FICTION / Social Issues / Drugs, Alcohol, Substance Abuse. | JUVENILE FICTION / Social Issues / Self-Esteem & Self-Reliance.
Classification: LCC PZ7.K94872 Sm 2016 | DDC [Fic]—dc23 LC record available at https://lccn.loc.gov/2015035869

1 2 3 4 5 6 7 8 9 10

Design by Kristin Logsdon
Text set in Arno Pro

For my November boys,
who have so many stories inside of them.
I can tell.

Character may almost be called the most effective means of persuasion.

—Aristotle

ALWAYS, ALWAYS . . .

You know what you're looking for. Age doesn't matter, but you're drawn to youth. It's your sentimentality, perhaps. Or the alluring knife-twist of nostalgia. That's a type of grief, isn't it? Pain from the past you're willing to relive, over and over and over again. It's the inevitable loss of yesterday.

It's the inevitable weight of more loss to come.

You don't have to do anything when you see her. That's the best part. The girl comes to you. You're seated in the crowded café, best table in the house. The one with the view of the gray skies outside. There are birds out there, too. There are blossoms on the trees.

There's also an empty chair right beside you. She asks to sit. You nod, and she sits and she tells you about herself. You knew she would. But you enjoy listening to her words. She's not dull or simpleminded, just filled with the false cynicism of her age. It's sweet, really. Like a rose who believes its thorns can keep it from being plucked. She's a college student, of course. An intellectual, she says with a blush. A deep thinker. She wants to be challenged. She wants more out of life.

It's almost too easy, this game you play. When the time comes to talk, you know the questions to ask. You know the things to say. Soon she's nodding. Soon she wants so much more of you.

That's how this story goes, my friend.

You know what you're looking for.

You know how to get it.

You always, always do.

1

ARMAN LOOKED OVER HIS SHOULDER and held his breath. His burning eyes squinted into the blinding Santa Cruz sun.

Besides a few palm trees, a jagged crack in the sidewalk, and a seagull pecking in the dirt, there was nothing in his immediate vicinity that he could see.

Nothing at all.

Sweat pooled in the small of his back. The air chafed his lungs. He turned to face forward again and kept walking. Using his right hand, Arman reached to adjust the nylon strap of the messenger bag he carried slung across his collarbone. It'd been gouging into his skin for a while, the strap, and shifting the bag's weight felt good. Well, not good, exactly, but *better*, since the absence of pain didn't imply pleasure.

All around Arman, the day shone bright, clear, and the air swelled ripe with brine and sea-rot the way it always did this close to the beach. He had nothing to worry about, he told himself. Not now. Not out in the open on a perfect summer day like this.

Right?

That's when Arman did it again. The looking-over-his-shoulder thing. He couldn't help it.

Still nothing. Just shadows. Sun. In the distance, tourists strolled the boardwalk, the pier. Surfers paddled in the water. The usual.

Arman felt silly about the way he was acting, like a spooked kid who believed monsters lived under his bed. But his heart disagreed. It pounded and pounded, going free-fall speed, *thud, thud, thud*, like it just might know something he didn't.

So he walked faster.

And faster.

By the time Arman made it over to the westside harbor, sweat was no longer pooling—it was pouring down his back. And his forehead. And the inside of his thighs. It felt like little rivulets of liquid had actually formed their own currents: merging and splitting and merging again as they ran to escape his body. Arman regretted not wearing shorts, even though he never wore shorts. And so with a sigh steeped in the banality of his own self-loathing, he ended up regretting that, too. The things that made him who he was.

Veering off the main road, Arman began the long march up the narrow path that led out toward the boulders and the waves at the end of the point. There was more wind here, a welcome relief from the late-morning heat, but the quick gusts off the ocean made his already itchy eyes sting with saline and his ears hum with the force of their roar.

He found them in the shadow of the lighthouse. Kira and Dale. It was where they'd been told to go, and they stood leaning against the tower's stone wall. More statues than teenagers. More dead than alive. They didn't look happy to see him, Arman noted as he drew closer. On the other hand, they didn't look *not* happy.

Just . . . neutral.

A fresh twinge of regret pinched at Arman's nerves, hard enough to bruise. Neutral was another way of saying he had *zero impact*. Neutral was another reminder of why he was here and, oh, what he was willing to give in order to change.

Which was just about *anything*.

Wasn't it?

Kira spoke first.

"Hey, kid," she said, reaching up to smooth her long braids.

Arman frowned. He was seventeen, like she was. In fact, he was eight months older than Kira, something he knew well, seeing as they'd gone to school together since the second grade. He figured she had to know it, too. And still, she had to go out of her way and say something like that, just to make him feel small.

Dale, on the other hand, said nothing. Just lifted his stubbled chin in greeting while keeping his hands in the pockets of his oversized shorts with the surf logo on the side. His mirrored sunglasses were pushed back on the top of his head and his eyes were bloodshot, which meant he was either stoned or hadn't slept. Or both.

"You ready to do this?" Arman's voice came out more tentative than he intended.

"You're not having doubts now, are you?" The intensity of Kira's gaze scorched him, made him squirm. For Arman, this was nothing new. Kira was about the hottest girl he knew, all soft lips and regal bones, always dressed in the kind of effortless clothes that teased of worlds he'd never know. Country clubs and art galleries. Dinner parties. Ivy League schools. Arman grew nervous whenever Kira looked right at him, despite the fact that she was black and he didn't go for black girls.

At least, he didn't think he did.

"No. No doubts," he said firmly. Gripping the messenger bag tighter to his body, Arman resisted the urge to peek over his shoulder again.

Forget small talk. This sucked, standing here. He wanted to get going, get started, get the hell out of this town. Once on the road, his paranoia would ease.

Wouldn't it?

"Yo," Dale said, in his lazy, soft-spoken way. Like he hadn't a care in the world. "They're here."

The passenger van sat idling in the lighthouse parking lot with its side door open. A welcome invitation and one they rushed toward. The van was white and it had five rows of bench seats with an aisle down the near side. Like a prison transport vehicle, Arman decided as he crawled in behind Dale. They could be San Quentin–bound or preparing to pick up trash off the side of the road, for all anyone watching them would know. It made about as much sense as what they were actually planning on doing.

A handful of adults, all middle-aged or older, none of whom Arman recognized, occupied the back of the vehicle. They looked nice enough, sort of friendly, open, with no obvious barriers to connection, but it wasn't like Arman could *really* tell. What people looked like sometimes told him what they might act like, but the correlation wasn't consistent enough for him to take any chances. He ducked his head and said nothing, sliding into an open seat as quickly as possible.

The man sitting next to the driver, at the front of the van, however, *was* someone Arman recognized. More than recognized. He was the reason Arman was here. The reason they were all here. The man's name was Beau, which was short for Beauregard, and Arman had met him precisely two weeks ago. While only the back of him was currently visible, Arman knew for a fact that Beau was tall and thin, with wide shoulders and eyes the color of river pebbles—slick and pale, first gray, then brown, then gray again. Staring at him, Arman felt a dizzying sway inside his stomach. Not from the motion of the van, which was nosing from the unpaved lot with its slow jolt and roll. No, this sway came from being in the presence of someone he respected. Admired, even. That had to be the word for the way he felt around Beau. This queasy mix of eagerness and hope. Like a listing ship just longing to be righted.

Beau glanced back only once, to survey the van's occupants. Arman tried smiling, eager for connection, but Beau's gaze passed him over. There was no warmth in his river-pebble eyes at the moment. Just curt appraisal. Maybe a hint of judgment.

He's busy, Arman reminded himself. *He's working. That's not a rejection. It's not personal.*

Because it really wasn't.

Right?

As the van picked up speed, heading for the highway, Arman started to relax. His body sank deeper into his seat, limbs loosening, mind quieting. He even let the messenger bag slip from his grasp to the floor with a soft *thunk,* as he shut his eyes, recalling the masterful way Beau had coached him on leaving home without arousing suspicion. Everything Beau had said worked perfectly. Like the proverbial charm. Two nights ago, Arman simply informed his mom that he was going camping in the mountains with some friends for the week. Deep down, he knew she didn't care. Deep down, he knew he could be leaving to join the rodeo clown circuit or train as a male escort, and she wouldn't lose an ounce of sleep worrying about his safety or well-being. Not so long as it meant her only child getting the hot fuck out of her sight and their non-air-conditioned POS Beach Flats apartment for a whole week of summer vacation.

The thing was, Arman's mom wasn't known for being rational. Or for acting in her own self-interest. No, she was known for her cynicism, the end result of a long string of disappointments that stretched back to before Arman was even born. Unfortunately for him, his mother's cynicism often came dressed as spite, so he'd braced himself for her resistance. The instant the words left his mouth, he just knew she was going to say no and cause a scene, determined not to suffer alone in her sweltering misery.

Only she hadn't.

Because Arman had *told* instead of asked.

Which was what Beau advised.

And now look. Look at him. He was free as a bird. Just like in that old song.

Well, *almost* free. Arman's gaze darted to the messenger bag at his feet. His stepfather, of course, was a different matter altogether. Arman had made his leaving and his freedom infinitely more complicated by getting that asshole involved.

2

THEY STOPPED FOR LUNCH JUST north of Big Sur, hiking down to picnic on a beach that was almost empty. The emptiness felt weird to Arman, who was used to crowds and surf wars and sand being kicked in his face—both metaphorical and otherwise. Without the usual cultural markers or territorial feuding, it felt as if they'd traveled farther than they really had. They could be in a different state, for all Arman knew. A different country. Or continent. Even in the gritty bathroom, one wretched and rank with the universal scent of human piss, the only thing that oriented him was the graffiti, which was written in both English and Spanish. All manners of obscenities and representations of female body parts were scrawled across the cement walls. One phrase in particular caught Arman's eye.

Daddy's farm.

He grimaced. Jesus. What the hell did *that* mean? Arman vaguely recalled a country song of the same name, but he didn't think that's what the words on the wall were referring to.

He zipped his pants and left the bathroom quickly.

Back in the warmth and clarity of the California sunshine, he strolled the water's edge, not caring if his shoes got wet. The waves were more wild here than back home in Santa Cruz. There was no cove. No harbor. No break wall. Just a relentless, pounding surf that made the ground shake with every roll and slam of its tide.

With some distance between him and the scene of his crime, Arman's paranoia waned from full throttle panic to a dull throb in his head. Now, when he glanced over his shoulder, Arman saw exactly what he expected to see: the distant forms of the van's other passengers, all eight of them, sprawled on blankets they'd dragged down to spread on the dry sand. Beau lay somewhat separate from the group, with his arms folded and sunglasses on. The rest of the passengers sat a few yards downwind, eating sandwiches, drinking sodas, talking, laughing, shooting the shit, whatever.

Arman's stomach growled, a useless plea. There was nowhere to buy food and he hadn't thought to bring any. Stupid, that was stupid of him. As always, he'd packed last minute, jamming his stuff into a single bag, with little forethought and a hell of a lot of impulsivity: rumpled clothes, a toothbrush, some deodorant, his acne wash, the medications he took for his ADHD and his GAD and his GERD and all the other acronyms that conspired to make his life as painful a disappointment as possible. Lastly, he threw in the book he was trying to finish, which was *Espedair Street* by Iain Banks. Arman had picked it up at one of those sidewalk sales downtown last spring. Although not a big reader, he found the first page made him cry right in the middle of Pacific Avenue, in front of strangers and everything. That felt meaningful somehow, like the words on the pages ached for him to know their sorrow.

He had money, too, of course, lots of it—$2,800 stolen from his meth-dealing stepfather, who no doubt owed it to his supplier, who no doubt would want it back at some point in time. Dread hooked his lungs at the thought—not because he believed stealing was wrong, which he did. And not because he cared about his stepfather, which he didn't. But because he cared about his mom. Sort of.

At least a little bit.

Stop. That's just a dumb symptom. Arman was determined to be better than that. He was determined not to bend to the will of guilt and shame. As hard it might be, he had to try—if not for himself, then for Beau, who believed he could do it. When they'd first met, by pure chance, at that music café in Capitola, the one overlooking a part of the ocean where the sea lions came to mate, Beau had talked to Arman, in his low sensible voice, about *self-defeating symptoms* and the ways they indicated sickness.

"I'm not sure I know what you mean," Arman had said, compelled to be honest in a situation where he'd normally lie.

Beau had smiled at him then, an expression as clear and easy to read as a full moon on a cloudless night. And there were no lines on his face. Not one. "Think about it this way. Just as a sneeze or a fever indicates an underlying infection in your body, wanting to please someone who's done nothing but neglect and abuse you is also a symptom."

"Of what?"

"Of *disease*. A man-made disease that feeds on your misery. Mark my words, Arman, your immune system has failed you. I can see it. There are cultural forces *right now* that are sucking the life out of your autonomy and happiness in order to thrive. They're no different from opportunistic bacteria and viruses that feed on their host. You're someone else's host. But you don't have to be."

That's when things had started to click for Arman. When he'd first felt that flicker-flame of hope. Autonomy and joy were scarce in his daily existence, only he'd never understood why. But now he had the answer: A disease was responsible. *Social order sickness*, Beau called it, or *the hierarchical flu*—both were the terms he used interchangeably to describe the sort of cultural syndrome that needed him to be weak in order for it to be strong. Apparently Arman had a pretty bad case of it. That's what the screening test Beau had given him said. And what he needed, Beau informed him, with those pale river eyes so full of compassion and understanding, was quarantine and recuperation.

Followed by *inoculation*.

Arman scooted sideways as a big wave washed in, shooting froth and bubbles at his feet. His dirty shoes slapped in the wetness and small crabs skittered in and out of holes and over rocks. He peeked at his phone. Five minutes before he had to board the van again. His stomach was still empty, a carved hollow, but his heart felt full, thinking of the days ahead, with all their promise and potential—a whole week spent at a private campground with Beau and other people like him, people who would teach Arman and Dale and Kira and all the other visitors who'd heard about Beau and what he could do, who understood that they needed help, too.

Who would he become? *What* could he become? Arman had no idea, but the future shimmered in front of him, so bright and vivid and *real*.

Giddy with his thoughts and the fresh ocean air, Arman reached down and picked up the tail end of a giant seaweed bulb that lay half buried in the sand. It had to be at least nine feet long. Cold and slimy, the thick green-brown tail slid around in his palm, but Arman held tight. He didn't let go. He began to jog, first stretching his legs and testing his muscles. Heavy sand weighted down his wet shoes and the damp cuffs of his jeans, but Arman forced his legs to go faster. He broke into a run, then a sprint, tugging hard on the seaweed tail. Behind him, the bulb head bounced and spun in the surf, like an eager kite that didn't yet know how to fly.

Back in the van, Dale sat in Arman's row for the last leg of the trip because Kira wanted to sleep. This meant sprawling her entire leggy body across the front row and Dale moving back, sunglasses, bloodshot eyes, surfer shorts and all. Arman slid in beside him but said nothing. He wasn't feeling unsocial, exactly, but he didn't know how to start a conversation and he didn't want to come off weird the way he always did. So he just slouched down. Held his book in his lap and hoped to God his stomach would stay quiet so Dale wouldn't ask why he hadn't eaten lunch with the rest of them.

The thing was, Arman and Dale weren't friends. They weren't anything. They'd only met each other once before, and that had been at the second gathering with Beau. Dale had shown up at the café that day, along with Kira, and that was when Beau invited them to the retreat. All dark hair and sloppy clothes and casual indifference, Dale had been aloof toward Arman then. Chilly, even. But in a way that made Arman long to know him. Or at least, not be dismissed by him.

That was another symptom, wasn't it? The longing. The need for acceptance and validation. The need for something other than himself, because he found himself lacking. Or maybe he *was* lacking and that's why he was needy? It was hard to tell the difference. Sometimes the symptom could be the cause. Arman leaned his head against the seat back and resisted the urge to slam it. *His* insecurities and failures were glaringly obvious, but what could Dale need? Dale was good-looking, athletic, emotionally tempered in ways Arman wished he could be. In other words, he was *cool*.

And yet he was here for a reason. He had to be.

Struggling to be sly about it, Arman lifted his head and side-eyed Dale as the van rocked and swayed, hugging the cliff-side curves on the twisting route southward. Interesting. Dale looked anything but aloof or cool now. He looked sick, actually. Sort of whey-faced and clammy, like the way Arman felt when he took too much Adderall. Dale was gripping the front of the van seat so hard the blood vessels in his hands were popping out. Blue ridges on white skin.

Arman nudged him with his foot. "Hey. You okay?"

Dale shook his head. His Adam's apple bobbed in his throat like a trapped frog. "I don't like heights."

Heights? A wave of sympathy washed over Arman. That was unfortunate, considering. Highway 1 definitely involved heights, lots of them: breathtaking, dizzying, unfathomable heights. It was a treacherous road, one that cut back and forth, inching along narrow drop-off cliffs and spanning stone bridges that floated high above the rocky shoreline and pounding waves. No guardrails stood between the road and oblivion, either. Arman kind of liked it that way: the view, the danger, the sheer sense of nail-biting awe. He'd heard that once a year a marathon ran up this road, and that a man in full tux and tails played a grand piano for the runners from atop one of these sharp-edged cliffs. He wanted to see that someday, a concert at the end of the world. It sent a thrill through him to think about it, to experience something so rare and fleeting. But for Dale there was clearly no upside to this.

Arman felt bad about that.

"You want to switch seats?" he offered. That way he'd be on the cliff side and Dale would only have a view of the oncoming traffic.

"No, I don't," Dale replied. "I don't want that at all."

Arman scowled. "Fine. I was just asking."

Dale folded his arms and let his heavy-lidded eyes flutter shut. "You know what I do want?"

"What?"

"What I want right now is some goddamn Klonopin."

"Klonopin?"

"Yeah."

"Well, sorry. All I've got is Paxil."

Dale's eyes popped open. "What did you say?"

"I said I have Paxil."

"What's Paxil?"

"It's an antidepressant. But it works for anxiety, too."

A smirk skittered across Dale's lips. "Seriously? You take that shit?"

Arman's shoulders tensed. "Why's it shit? You just said you wanted Klonopin."

"That's different."

"How's it different?"

Dale waved a hand. "It just is. Anyway, I heard they don't allow your kind of medication in this place. So you better watch out. Your Paxil's about to become a controlled substance."

"Why wouldn't they allow medication?"

"I don't know. Supposedly it *inhibits your experience of reality* or some bullshit. It was in a brochure I saw. Sounds pretty stupid, if you ask me. Reality's what we make of it, right?"

Arman felt weak. He had no idea what reality was or wasn't. He also didn't care. What he *did* care about was not breaking rules. He didn't want to get in trouble. He didn't want to do anything he wasn't supposed to.

But he needed his medication.

He turned to Dale. "You know, I meant what I said about switching seats."

"Hell, sure. Why not." Dale gestured for Arman to stand up, which he did. Dale scooted toward the aisle while Arman wriggled toward the window. And even though he still held his book in his lap, he didn't read or relax. He sat up straight for the rest of the ride.

They pulled into the campground a little before four.

Their van was one of at least a dozen in the gravel parking area. There were a couple of trucks, too, and an ATV, and even an old dust-covered sailboat that looked like it hadn't seen water in half a century.

Stepping out and gazing at the steep-pitched hills around him, Arman realized *campground* wasn't the most accurate word. To him it had conjured up images of tents and bug bites and shitting in the woods, which were all things he remembered from the times his dad had taken him camping, usually up near Tahoe. Those were trips that had taken place years ago. They'd also grown less enjoyable over time; the older Arman got, the more comfortable his dad grew with abandoning him while he frequented the South Lake casinos. Arman hated being left alone in those scummy campgrounds, surrounded by bikers and drunks and the constant reek of pot smoke. But this place was different. This place, rooted deep in a desolate section of the central coastal range, wound in on a dirt road, through miles of lost canyons, miles from anywhere, and ringed on every side by some sort of geological barrier, felt more like a *compound.*

First off, this was clearly private property. The hand-lettered sign on the wrought-iron scroll gate they'd driven through said as much. There were other signs, as well. One read NO TRESPASSING and another KEEP OUT, but the most curious message was the one carved into the metal archway that ran above the massive barred gate. Arman had had to lean to see it, twisting his head against the van's window, but what he saw read:

EVOLVE

ALIA TENTANDA VIA EST

Arman knew that was Latin. It sounded familiar, too, only he didn't know what it meant, other than the *evolve* part. He couldn't even look up the rest of the phrase because there was no cell service here. There hadn't been for the last hour of the drive.

The van's other passengers streamed past Arman and up a cobblestone path. Only Beau wasn't with them. He wasn't anywhere. Arman's heart stuttered as he glanced around. *Crap.* Apparently Arman's daydreaming had made him miss something important. Again. He gripped his bag and hurried after the rest of the group. He was determined to pay attention from now on. He just had to focus. He just had to be a better person.

They headed toward a large domed structure that had been built into the hillside. Wood smoke puffed from the dome's chimney. And that was another thing that made this place a not-campground. Instead of tents, there were buildings, real buildings. Lots of them—from what Arman could make out—all made of wood, red where raw, but weathered silver. Beyond the dome was a large meadow ringed with small cabins and other outbuildings. Even farther, pine and cypress trees dotted the thicketed landscape, and dirt trails twined and vanished into a dark forest that stretched as far as the eye could see.

Breathing in the sharp scent of eucalyptus leaves and wafting licorice bushes that lined the path he was on, Arman's heart continued to rattle, not just with nerves, but excitement, too. His allergies had already receded in the few minutes he'd been here, and whatever "*alia tentanda via est*" meant and whatever kind of place this happened to be, at least it was *different*. Here he could be someone new. Here he had no history of embarrassing himself or not making friends or being the weird, sickly one-off sheep no one thought was interesting or valuable enough to look for when he inevitably wandered off, lost inside his own head.

At least, not yet.

Arman snuck one last peek over his shoulder. He gave a long stare back down the dirt hill drive toward the iron gate, but it was too far away for him to see, and this realization calmed him, dousing whatever was left of the paranoia he'd generated by stealing from his stepfather and running away. Because not being able to see the gate meant he couldn't see where he'd come from.

And *that* meant, for the very first time in his entire seventeen years of life, Arman believed he might actually be safe.

3

BEFORE HE COULD STEP INSIDE the domed building to join the others, Beau pulled him aside.

"C'mere," he said, appearing from nowhere to place a hand on Arman's shoulder, steering him away from the flow of foot traffic and out toward the meadow. He'd changed clothes, which confused Arman. When had that happened? No longer dressed in jeans and the thin button-down shirt he'd been wearing during the van ride, Beau was now in all beige—still pants and a shirt, but the style wasn't one Arman had ever seen before. The clothes he wore were sort of loose and flowy. Like they were built for a different climate.

"Is everything okay?" Arman asked. Walking in Beau's longer shadow, he felt lacking. Insufficient. Had he already been judged unworthy of being here? Beau had invited him after only meeting him twice and so it was definitely possible he'd made a mistake. Maybe now he needed to fix that mistake by asking Arman to leave.

Shut up. That's the zero effect *talking.*

Maybe so, but why was he being singled out? Where was Kira? And Dale?

Arman started to do the thing he always did when he felt like he'd disappointed somebody.

He began to sweat, in all sorts of terrible places.

And he picked at his arm, gouging his skin with his nail.

Beau stepped down into a garden of some kind. Arman made himself follow. Grass crunched underfoot and the garden was lush, bright, filled with the flowery scent of summer and the sleepy buzz of the dragonflies and the soft burbling of a cool, stone fountain. Beau talked to Arman as they walked, murmuring about self-sufficiency and pointing out things like a knotted grove of apple trees and growing tubs for herbs and a reverse irrigation drip system that could double their crop of heirloom tomatoes and even a whole cluster of white-lidded beehives, but Arman wasn't catching his words. Not really. His mind wouldn't focus. He kept picking at his arm, digging deeper. Everything felt fuzzy.

". . . very glad you're here," he heard faintly. Then: "Arman? *Arman?*"

He dropped his hands to his sides. Felt the sticky ooze of blood and prayed Beau didn't notice. "Yeah?"

"You okay, son?"

"Yeah, I'm fine. Just a little hungry, I think. I feel kind of dizzy."

"Did you eat lunch?"

"No." Arman blushed more. Harder. Hotter. Whatever. He was too embarrassed to admit he'd forgotten to pack himself food. Who *did* that?

"I'll take you to the kitchen, then," Beau said firmly. "I'm sure the cook will be able to find something to hold you over until dinner. Can't have you getting sick or malnourished while you're out here, okay?"

Arman nodded. The pounding of his heart slowed and his mind cleared. So he wasn't being asked to leave before even really arriving?

That was good. That was definitely good. He pushed his shaggy hair back and squinted up at Beau.

With a hint of silver dotting his temple, the older man had a kind face. A normal one, too. He didn't have a pervy smile like that basketball coach back in middle school who was always trying to give him a ride home, or the pissed-off glare of Arman's stepfather who never wanted him around. He didn't even have the canary-eating-cat sneakiness Arman had learned to read in the seemingly placid face of his real father. There was just a presence about Beau. Something intangible. And honest. He exuded warmth without being sappy. Strength without being uncaring.

"Look," Beau said. "I wanted to prepare you for some things before we go in there. Before we really *get started.*" He gestured toward the domed building.

"Oh, okay," Arman said, although he wanted to ask, *Get started on what?*

"You know, you being here. It's something special. For me."

"It is?"

"Absolutely. The others who are here, well, they're paying a lot of money to learn what my program can teach them. It's knowledge we want to share, obviously, but to do that, we have to have a system. Our research must be funded. Maintained. You understand that, right?"

Arman nodded again, but the shakiness in his legs returned. Research? Maintaining a system? He was only saying he understood because he didn't want to be perceived as stupid, but that's pretty much what he was. He was bone clueless about whatever the hell Beau was talking about. He had a sinking feeling Beau knew it, too.

His eyes widened with sudden awareness. "Wait," he said. "I can pay you. Is that what this is about? Kira said it was fifteen hundred for the week, and I've got that. I've got more, if you want it. I never intended not to pay!" With that, he slipped the messenger bag off his shoulder and onto the ground. Dropped to his knees to rifle through it. He'd wrapped the stolen bills in newspaper, then plastic, before stuffing them in the very bottom, beneath his clothes.

"Arman, stop."

"Huh?"

"That's what I wanted to tell you." Beau knelt beside him in the grass, the warmth of the late-day sun flooding over them both. The bees hummed louder. A woodpecker hammered at a tree above them. "I don't want your money, okay?"

"You don't?"

"No."

Arman froze, confused. "Why not?"

"For one, you can't afford it. However you got that money in your bag, well, I don't want to know. Two, it's important to me that you're here. Critical, actually."

Arman opened his mouth. He wanted to say that he *could* afford to pay. Of course he could. He'd risked so much to come here, it didn't seem right not to use the money he'd stolen from his stepfather. It didn't seem right that his sacrifice had been in vain.

But Beau kept talking, kept using that slow, soporific voice of his. "I need something good this summer, Arman. Something I care about. There's been discord here, of late, I'm afraid. A certain ugliness. In fact, there's someone at the compound right now intent on destroying the life I've worked so hard to build."

"I'm sorry to hear that," Arman said. He meant it, too.

Beau's expression grew solemn. "You know, when I was a teenager, I was a lot like you. Trapped in a bad place without even understanding how bad it was. My mother was an unhappy person and her unhappiness poisoned me. Made me scared of the world. Scared of myself, actually."

"And your dad?" Arman ventured. Then he held his breath.

Beau plucked a stem of clover from the ground. Cupped it in the palm of his hand. "My father was worthless. Utterly worthless. When he was around, all he did was tell lies. And not good lies. Awful ones. The kind that let you know that things can always be worse. The kind that let you know some fathers were never meant to have sons."

Arman felt dizzy again. He couldn't believe what he was hearing. Beau was confiding in *him*. That felt important. More than important, it felt significant.

Beau leaned closer then. Until their foreheads almost touched. "You can't tell anyone about our arrangement, though. Inequality breeds unrest. At least at this part of the process."

"Oh, sure. Of course."

"Later it'll be different. Later they'll understand that self-comparison is the medium in which illness is incubated. But now, not so much."

"I see," Arman said, although he didn't see. Not at all.

But clearly he'd said the right thing, because Beau nodded, relieved, standing again to rock back on his heels. "Life isn't fair, of course, but sometimes the illusion of equity is necessary. This is one of those times."

"Um, yeah."

"So I can trust you, Arman? To be discreet? And to take full advantage of this opportunity?"

Now Arman nodded vigorously. He could do both of those things. He would. And by not spending the stolen money, well, maybe that meant doing something else when he left here. Like not going back home. Ever.

He smiled up at Beau. He felt good. The two of them had a secret.

"Thanks," he said. "Thanks a lot."

Beau smiled back.

———

The kitchen was located in a building adjacent to the dome and the sweet-smelling garden. Beau and Arman entered through a sliding glass door. The room was large. Impressive. Ceiling fans cooled the air and the whole space was filled with spinning light and warm smells and chipped terra-cotta tiles.

Arman gazed around. Saw long stainless steel counters and double sinks. Even a walk-in freezer. How many people did they plan on feeding? How many people were actually *here*? There'd been nine of them total in the van, but then he remembered all the other vans, plus the cabins and the buildings. Beau murmured something about the dining room being through a pair of swinging doors, but Arman wasn't paying attention. He was too busy watching the cook, a young woman in a yellow dress made of the same gauzy material as Beau's clothing. She moved with an ease that made Arman embarrassingly aware of how tight his own clothes were. She also had bare legs and bright eyes that stared right back at Arman when Beau asked her to feed him.

She nodded. But she didn't take her eyes off Arman.

"I'm needed in the meeting hall now," Beau told her. "Please send Arman back when he's finished."

She nodded again, and with that he slipped away.

Arman sat shyly at the table the cook gestured him toward. She smiled at him when she did this. Or at least he thought it was a smile—a slight twitch of her lips that looked effortless, the way a ladybug might flap her wings. She poured iced tea from a large pitcher she took from the refrigerator and set a full glass in front of him.

"Thank you," Arman said, gripping the glass, absorbing its chill. Thick slices of lemon and mint leaves floated among the ice cubes.

The cook didn't respond. She turned away from him and returned to her work. Despite her silence, the room was filled with sound: Soft music spilled from speakers mounted on a bare wood shelf, and the atmosphere in the kitchen was peaceful, both drowsy and dreamy. Arman leaned his thin shoulders against the wall and gazed out at the meadow and the woods and drank the tea, slow sip by even slower sip. It tasted sweet.

It tasted like what he needed.

A plate appeared before him moments later. Simple food. Chunks of cheese, warm bread, slices of fresh fruit, roasted almonds, and a few drizzles of honey, all neatly laid out on a heavy ceramic plate. Arman stared. Then realized he was *starving*. He ate fast, using his hands, wolfing down the bread and honey first, followed by the almonds, lightly salted. Next he devoured the fruit: raspberries, blueberries, blackberries—all sweet as a miracle, they must have come from the garden—sitting alongside chunks of pink melon and the tiniest grapes he'd ever seen. Sugary juice ran down Arman's chin, his wrists, stinging a bit as it hit the patch of raw skin on his forearm, and he winced, forced to pause in his gluttony—a reluctant temperance—before continuing with his meal. Slower this time.

The cheese he only nibbled at, out of caution not distaste. Last year he'd been diagnosed with lactose intolerance—along with GERD— and while cheese didn't usually give him problems, it wasn't worth the risk or the pain.

Arman didn't much like risk.

Or pain.

So he left most of the cheese uneaten. That was fine. Sated and satisfied, Arman figured he should get himself to the meeting hall. Join the group. But sitting there, stomach full and stretched comfortably, with the drowsiness in his limbs and the good music playing over the speakers, soothing his soul, well, he didn't *want* to leave. He was not unaware that this was the first time in a long while that anyone had taken care of him.

It felt nice.

But it couldn't last, could it? Nothing good did. Besides, he needed to do what he'd promised Beau: take advantage of this opportunity. That meant getting his butt to the meeting. He didn't need to fall any farther behind than he already was.

Pushing his chair back, Arman spurred his body into motion. He gathered the plate and glass, and walked over to the work area where the cook was washing lettuces and shucking ears of summer corn. It was strange, he thought, her being the only one here.

"Thank you," he said again, setting the dishes down on the counter by the sink.

The cook whirled to face him. She stared, her eyes narrowed, her brows knitted tight. It was like he'd startled her. Like she'd forgotten his very presence. Wisps of loose hair fell onto her cheeks, her neck.

Am I really here? Can she see me?

"Sorry," Arman said meekly. "I didn't mean to scare you."

She continued to stare. She wasn't much older than he was, maybe college-aged, and she was pretty in a quiet way. It was the dress, perhaps. Or her kindness.

Arman squirmed. Tried to take a step backward. "I should go."

The cook came toward him then, still silent but no longer quiet. No, she was bold in her approach. Imperious. Chin lifted, she stopped right in front of him, mere millimeters away. Arman froze. He'd never been this close to a girl, not alone and not ever, and he had no idea what she wanted. He had no idea where to look. A part of him hoped she couldn't smell him—all that sweating he'd done earlier, *God*—and Arman's lungs constricted, sinking into a breathless knot, as the hairs on his arms rose up in an effort to reach her. Like flowers bending toward the sun.

"Is something wrong?" he whispered. "Did I do something wrong?"

The cook's response was to lean forward and press her lips to his. She proceeded to do this, very gently, while at the same time shoving one hand down the front of his pants.

At her touch, Arman made a noise. An odd one. Part fear. Part longing. But the cook kept kissing him, kept pushing her tongue around inside his mouth. It was a sensation as invasive as it was pleasurable, a probing wetness that addled his brain while what she did with her hand down lower—all confidence and expertise—sent jolts of electricity through his stomach. His chest. His limbs.

His *everything*.

Then the cook was making him move—pulling his jeans off, pulling him to the floor, pulling her own dress up over her head so that Arman could see what was beneath. Skin and softness and patches of downy hair. He finally ventured to reach between her legs, a timid approach, because it seemed like what she wanted him to do, but the slippery heat he felt there was almost too much. Somehow the cook knew this. Maybe it was the way his legs trembled. Or the new noise he was making. She pushed his hand away. Got on top of him.

Realizing what she was going to do, what they were *already* doing and what would soon be over, Arman couldn't help himself. This was the second time in one day that someone was giving him something. A gift he hadn't earned. That had never happened before, and he had to know.

"Why?" he gasped. "Why are you doing this?"

The cook leaned down, her body devouring his with little to no temperance at all, and she whispered three words.

Words Arman never thought he'd hear.

She said to him:

I need you.

4

ARMAN WONDERED IF THEY COULD smell it on him. Or if they saw something different in the way he walked or the way he talked or the way he just *was*. But if Kira and Dale happened to notice anything at all about him, they kept it to themselves, simply walking side by side and going on about the meeting he'd missed. Arman trailed behind, trying to listen. But he felt dazed.

He felt distant.

To the west, the sun faded quickly, dipping below trees, and slipping behind hill after hill after hill toward the ocean beyond. Apparently Kira and Dale were heading toward the cabin where they'd be rooming for the duration of the retreat. Only they knew the way. Arman had run into them as he left the kitchen, slinking out through the sliding glass door, and walking . . . well, more like *stumbling* back through the garden, past the drooping vines of honeysuckle and the apple orchard and the beehives, drained, jelly-legged, and no longer innocent.

Wasn't that something?

"Come on," they'd called to him, pausing and waving from the main path. "You're staying with us."

Staying where? Arman had wanted to ask, hating how clueless he was, but instead he'd said nothing. He was still too stunned by what had transpired between him and the bare-legged cook, the young woman in the yellow dress who'd fed him and then—

Arman's whole body shuddered at the memory.

In a good way.

Mostly.

"We're sleeping in *here*? Together?" Kira frowned. They stood huddled in the screened doorway of the tiny single-room cabin. Three cots with crisp white sheets were pushed together against the back wall. Three glasses, a flashlight, and a pitcher of water sat on a small round table. A bare-bulb light swung from the center beam, giving the place a stark, haunted feel.

Dale walked in first, his shoes kicking up dust. Then he shrugged. "Yeah. I guess so."

Kira still balked. "Why aren't I bunking with the girls? Isn't there some sort of, I don't know, *protocol*?"

Dale let out a low chuff of laughter. He sank onto the closest cot. The springs squeaked loudly beneath his weight. As if they, too, were unpleasantly surprised by the sleeping arrangements. "Protocol," he echoed. "Yeah, right. Everything they said in that meeting was so vague, who knows what we're meant to be doing? We're here to change, because change is needed. We'll find answers when we stop asking questions. So maybe the protocol is no protocol. Maybe we're supposed to spend our nights having some sort of freaky threesome with Arman here while all the old shits get off by watching us. Maybe that's the damn protocol."

Arman felt flush. The mere mention of sex so soon after what he'd just done, it was almost more than he could handle.

"I don't think that's what we're supposed to do," Kira told Dale.

He shrugged. "Did you see anyone else in that room you're dying to sleep next to? Anyone within two decades of your age?"

Kira grinned and shook her head. Then she bounded across the room on those long legs of hers, leaping and soaring to land on top of Dale with a laugh.

"No," she said, staring down at him. "I didn't see anyone else I'd want to sleep next to. Those people, they were all . . . all . . ."

"All what?" Arman asked from where he still stood in the doorway, digging at his arm with his finger.

Kira lifted her head. "I don't know. I guess they were nothing special. That's what they were. They were ordinary. A bunch of ordinary old folks."

"Well, what else happened at the meeting?"

"We already told you what happened," Kira said. "Where were you anyway?"

Arman dug harder. "I needed to take care of something."

"Hmph." She didn't look convinced.

"I'll tell you what we did. We had to take an oath of secrecy." Dale held up three fingers like a Boy Scout. "And we had to promise to do every single thing our trainers tell us to do. Or else."

"Or else what?" Arman asked.

"You get kicked out, I guess. Or maybe worse. They have security guards, you know. Armed ones. Maybe you'll end up in an unmarked grave."

Arman gaped. "Armed guards?"

"They did *not* have guns," Kira said.

"Yes, they did," Dale scoffed. "Of course they did. They need guns to keep us here, because this place is about *Freedom* and *Discovery* and embarking on your *Personal Journey*. As if there isn't enough horseshit in this world already."

Kira winked at Arman. "He's just pissed because he can't smoke weed."

"We'll see about that." Dale slapped her ass then. Kira giggled, returned the favor, slapping even harder, and Arman looked away. Sure, he'd known they were dating or hooking up or whatever. Or at least he'd guessed that might be the case. It hadn't been anything he'd cared much about. Only now, having to live with them, well, that made him a third wheel, didn't it? Arman crossed the room and threw his bag down with a huff. Then he dragged one of the cots as far away from the other two as possible.

Kira watched him keenly, her eyes bright. "You're blocking the door," she pointed out.

"I know," Arman said. He sat on his cot and kept his back to the other two. The windows to the cabin were open and he stared out at the vast California sky that was just beginning to purple. A heaviness settled in his chest and the warm glow memory of those brief gasping moments with the bare-legged cook was already starting to fade into something less magical and far more profane. More *ordinary*. It was the kind of heaviness Arman was used to, this steamrolling weight that knew how to press the joy out of him, inch by inch.

Reaching to pick his forearm again, he tried telling himself to appreciate what he had and the chance he'd been given. That his time here wouldn't be anything like the lonely month he'd spent at that Gold Rush–themed sleepaway camp his father's parents paid to send him to back in seventh grade. His first night there, a nervous stomach kept him in the infirmary and by the time he rejoined his cabin, it was too late; everybody already had their friends and understood the rules. He was nothing but a burden. An understudy. Something to resent for daring to exist. Not that *he* was any better, of course. Arman was rotten that same summer to a girl who liked him because she had hairs on her chin and talked too much about Jesus. But maybe that was just how the world was, he thought.

Maybe everything was rotten.

When he turned around again, Kira and Dale weren't fucking or anything. What they were doing was lying face-to-face and gazing into each other's eyes. And not talking. Somehow that was infinitely worse than fucking. Arman tried to avoid looking at them while he scanned the rest of the cabin—he wanted to find one of those brochures Dale had talked about—but he couldn't take it. He got up and left. The screen door swung shut behind him with a bang.

Arman went in search of a bathroom. There had to be one, he figured, since there was electricity and plumbing and the compound clearly wasn't lacking in amenities, except things like privacy and general social norms. He was right, too, because after hiking a little ways up the hillside, and passing another small cluster of cabins, along with a long, institutional-looking two-story building that had dark windows and no signs of life, he found the washroom. It was an A-frame structure, nestled tight in a ring of pine trees.

Arman walked right in, daring to hope against hope that there might be a good supply of hot water for the showers. That was what was needed to clear his head. Steam. Heat. A thorough cleansing.

What he found, however, was far less pleasing—an open space lit by skylights, where a half-naked woman sat on a wooden bench, one leg hitched over the other, clipping her toenails. A towel was wrapped around her waist, but not her top half, and she had to be at least his grandmother's age, if not older. Her thick gray hair dripped water everywhere, like an over-soaked sponge.

Arman was so mortified he thought he might die right there on the spot. "I'm so sorry," he sputtered, squeezing his eyes shut and backpedaling himself into a wall with a bang. But it was too late. The woman was balanced perfectly on the bench so that the late-day sun poured down on her like a spotlight, and he'd already seen more than he should have. *Way* more. Wrinkled skin, sagging tits, age spots. The whole damn mess.

Even worse, the old woman roared with laughter at his reaction. "Don't be sorry," she said. "This is your bathroom, too."

"It is?" he asked, partially opening his eyes, but keeping them glued to the sealed cement floor.

"It is."

"I don't understand."

The woman stood, a move that took both time and effort on her part, and which didn't involve her covering up. Then she came toward him. Watching her wet, bare, bunioned feet approach, Arman's stomach lurched. For a panicked instant he thought she was going to do what the cook had done to him in the kitchen. Pull him to her. Rub her hips against his. Undo the button on his jeans and grab on to him with an eagerness he'd be helpless to resist.

But she didn't. Instead, the old woman reached out and patted his arm. Her skin was very soft. Arman lifted his head to look at her, still abashed, still blushing, but wanting so badly to be brave.

She smiled. "Maybe you can understand living a life where what other people think doesn't rule your actions."

Arman tried smiling back, returning some of her warmth, but he couldn't help blurting out, "I don't, though. That's just it. I don't understand anything about that."

"You will," she told him gently. "*Soon.*"

SOMEDAY.

You see the girl again and nothing's changed. Sure, she doesn't smile as much. And this time she's the one asking the questions. She's determined to be assertive now, to take charge, and you like that. She doesn't know that this is the way it always goes. She doesn't know that you need her doubt before her conviction.

You meet at a park this time. The nice one off Soquel that's not far from the beach. Lots of students lie in the well-kept grass, reading quietly, soaking up sun. You can tell the most studious types by the paleness of their skin and the way they roll their pant cuffs. They're also the ones smoking cigarettes, not joints, and women with children throw dirty looks their way.

She wants to know what you think about religion. She was raised Jewish, but she doesn't believe. Or she doesn't want to. This is causing friction with her family. What she wants is the freedom to make her own choices. To find her own path toward spirituality. You smile at this and say the things you always say. That she's having the right kinds of thoughts, but that she's looking for the wrong kinds of answers. That religion isn't a matter of right or wrong. It's a matter of now and then.

Faith is an investment, you tell her, when you see she doesn't understand. You bargain now for what you hope matters then.

The girl laughs, not because you're right, but because she thinks you're clever. You don't push it more than that. Instead, you switch gears, asking about her friends at school. If there are other people on campus as smart as she is. Not as smart, she says, and this time you both laugh. Then you enjoy the sunshine for a bit, which feels good. She doesn't smoke, like the other students. You comment on this, in a positive sort of way. Seems like an easy enough thing to do, but at your words she frowns and looks elsewhere. You're intrigued by this. More than intrigued. You've hit on something. A tenderness. You'll be sure to remember that.

It will be useful to you someday.

5

"SO WHERE ARE YOU FROM?" a voice asked.

"Huh?" Arman lifted his head and looked around. It was nighttime now, almost nine o'clock, and he was seated at a dinner table, surrounded by three strangers, in a room lit by candle glow. He wasn't eating, because there wasn't any food. What he *was* doing, however, was surreptitiously shaking two pills around in his hand, while weighing the pros and cons of taking them. One was his pink oval-shaped Paxil, which had to be taken with meals. The other was one of his short-acting Adderalls.

"I asked where you were from," the voice said again, and it was Mari speaking to him, the old woman he'd met in the bathroom just hours earlier. Now fully dressed, she sat across from him, with her hair neatly braided, her soft face shadowy in the jumpy light.

Arman decided that he liked Mari. He really did. The whole naked thing wasn't that big a deal, and whatever kind of deal it was, well, that was on him. Not only had she been gracious this afternoon, she'd helped him out again when he'd shown up in the dining room alone after not being able to find Kira and Dale back in the cabin. In fact, Arman would've missed the meal altogether if he hadn't seen the stream of people walking past his open window and decided to join them, following along in silence until he reached the dining hall, this cavernous room so completely different from the bright and sunny kitchen he'd eaten in earlier. No, this space, filled with heavy drapes and low-hanging candelabras, was grim and foreboding—full of secrets and dark wood, hushed tones and the rich scent of burning incense.

Arman had been lost in the swell of strangers—there had to be at least a hundred people here, some dressed in those light gauzy clothes, others not—and he'd stood frozen by the entryway, like a sweaty-palmed zombie. In fact, he stood there so long, he'd started to imagine the aging, blond bodyguard-looking guy who was staring at him from across the room was plotting to drag him out back and put him out of his misery. The guy could've definitely been one of the guards Dale had mentioned, only Arman had no clue how to tell if someone was armed. He had no clue about anything, a fact made blatantly obvious when Mari had come up to him, taken his arm, and guided him to her table. There, she'd poured him a glass of red wine and shushed him when he said he wasn't old enough to drink.

"You know, you're not supposed to ask him that," the woman next to Mari scolded. She was younger than Mari, but still old. Maybe the same age as Arman's mom. Forty something? He couldn't tell. She had long black hair and brown skin and an accent he couldn't place.

Arman closed his fist around his pills. "Why aren't you supposed to ask me where I come from?"

"Drink your wine," Mari instructed. "You're too tense."

Obedient as always, Arman picked up the glass and drank his wine. It tasted funny. Not sweet like how it smelled, but acidy and thick. Almost gritty. He drank more, gulped it really, wondering if he would get drunk from one glass. Being drunk wasn't something he had a lot of experience with, although that wasn't innocence born from any moral compass, but rather a lack of opportunity.

A short man on Arman's left leaned in. "You're new here, right? Just came in today?"

"Yes."

"Well see, then that's why you don't know."

"Know what?"

"That we're not supposed to talk about our lives from before. Not at first. This is a place for rebirth. For rejuvenation. We make our own stories here. They don't make us."

"Oh," Arman said.

"Quarantine's not until tonight," Mari called from across the table. "He's still whoever he is until then. There's nothing wrong with asking."

The man shrugged, and Arman wanted to be the one to ask more questions, like what happened at Quarantine and who would make his story and how could he possibly be anyone but who he already was? But the food came then, hot and steamy and aromatic, and the time for asking disappeared into the vapor.

A table to their left got up to serve, six figures slipping into the kitchen through an open doorway and returning with various dishes. Arman got to his feet to help, too, in part because he wanted to go into the kitchen and see if things were how he remembered them, but Mari gave a shake of her head, her lips forming a frown, and he quickly sat again.

Heaping bowls of wild rice and hot platters of roast chicken with buttery potatoes appeared on the table, along with warm rolls wrapped in towels and savory oven-roasted vegetables and green salad and peach chutney. A feast, practically. Arman's eyes grew wider and wider. He'd never seen a meal this big, except maybe that dinner he'd had the year he'd spent a disastrous Thanksgiving with his father's family up in Marin.

The last thing to be served, a bowl of sweet corn sprinkled with mint, was set directly in front of Arman. At this he glanced up to see the cook standing there, right beside him, very close. Still in her yellow dress.

Still with her bare legs and soft hair pulled off her neck.

She nodded, giving Arman a quick tip of her head before moving her gaze downward, toward his hand. The one holding the pills. He shoved it under the table.

"Hey," he said.

The cook didn't answer. Instead she brushed against him, like a cat to a corner or an uncrossed knee, and whether that was by accident or design, he didn't know. After that, she simply floated away, disappearing into the depths of the room. Arman watched her go with a deep sense of both longing and loss. It wasn't until she'd vanished beyond the reach of candlelight that he shifted his attention back to the table. Realized everyone was staring at him.

Arman cleared his throat. Turned to the short man beside him.

"So, uh, what happens tonight?" he asked. "The Quarantine thing? Can you tell me more about that?"

"Weren't you at the meeting earlier?" The man handed him the platter of chicken. "It was explained there."

"Well, yes," Arman lied. "Of course I was there."

The dark-haired woman sniffed. "You don't seem to know very much."

"Sorry. I sort of space out a lot." Arman resisted the urge to pick at his arm. He set about searching for a piece of dark meat. Found the smallest one.

"You have to be engaged at all times," Mari told him. "Once sessions begin, we'll expect you to retain everything you've been taught. You can't evolve without awareness. It's not possible."

"We don't suffer fools here," the short man said with a grunt.

"Or tolerate ignorance," finished the dark-haired woman.

"Sessions," Arman said slowly, realizing these three must be the trainers Dale had talked about. "Sessions that you all help teach."

"That's right." Mari gave him a warm smile. She was holding the basket of rolls. Arman watched her take two.

"What about Beau?" he asked.

"What about him?"

"I thought this was his program. His, you know, community."

Mari's smile grew broader. "A community doesn't belong to any one person. It belongs to all of us."

"So it's not his?"

"You know, I think what would serve you best right now," she said, "is to focus on your own experience. Growth can happen when and where you least expect it."

Arman nodded. "Yeah. Sure. Okay. I can do that."

She practically glowed. "Wonderful. Now would you please pass the butter?"

"So who's on your list?" the dark-haired woman asked the short man, who was busy fingering his wispy comb-over while draining a second glass of wine.

"There's a couple that came in today," he said with a smack. "Retired. No children. Nice house in Malibu."

"Anyone else?"

"Don't know yet. The rest are Beau's, so I doubt it."

"What are you talking about?" Arman couldn't help but interrupt. But it wasn't like their conversation was private. He could hear everything.

The dark-haired woman glanced over at him. "Oh, we're just making our predictions," she said.

"Predictions about what?"

But the woman didn't answer. Instead she leaned forward, edging her chair closer to the short man and laughing before whispering something into his ear. And this time, when she spoke, Arman couldn't hear a word she said.

After the meal came dessert—some sort of spice cake—followed by hot tea with milk and nutmeg. Feeling like he was being judged and undoubtedly failing, Arman made sure to eat everything and drink everything, despite the fact he was starting to feel uncomfortably full. Drowsy, too, his neck turning laggy under the descending weight of sleep pressure. He was exhausted. More than exhausted, having spent the previous night tossing in bed, worrying about leaving home, worrying about getting the money from his stepfather's safe, worrying about what would happen to his mother when his stepfather found out, worrying about *everything*. At the memory, a surge of anxiety threatened to bubble into his consciousness, but Arman shut his eyes. Strained to push it all away.

You're safe now. You're free.

Then Mari was standing behind him, shaking him gently.

"It's time to go," she whispered, and Arman blinked, confused. When had she gotten up? When had everybody? He looked around. The dining hall was practically empty, people quietly streaming out, their chairs pushed back, piles of dishes and glassware left in their wake. What was going on? *God.* Had he been *sleeping*?

"Go where?" he asked Mari.

"The meeting hall," she said. "It's time."

———

Arman swallowed his pills before he left. Mari went on ahead, and he did it when no one was looking, deftly slipping the Paxil and Adderall into his napkin, pressing the whole thing to his lips, and downing a mouthful of water while he got to his feet.

He didn't look back as he walked toward the door. He felt guilty about taking the pills and he hated that. The guilt made him feel like he was trying to get away with something rather than keeping himself from falling apart. It wasn't just the rule-breaking that made him feel this way, either. It was the way he always felt, thanks to countless lectures from teachers fretting over his "wasted potential" and years of living with a father who believed ADHD and nerves and stomachaches were all signs of weakness, true failures in character. Like *he* was one to talk. Mikhail Dukoff's current reality was the type of failure Arman was doing his damnedest never to experience.

Of course, Arman also understood medication couldn't *fix* his problems. Not the things that truly haunted him, like why he couldn't connect to others and why he hated himself for that. But the pills helped. They were all he had. They cleared his head and calmed his nerves, and they held him together the way a plastic bag might hold the pieces of a jigsaw puzzle that had long since lost their box.

6

ARMAN WAS HALFWAY UP THE trail to the meeting hall when someone came sprinting up behind him. With no warning at all. Before he could turn to look over his shoulder, the person flew past, grabbing for his arm as they went. Whoever it was tried dragging Arman along, pulling him into a run. He was willing to go, only his body did things all wrong. He took one step only to have his shoes tangle, throwing him to the ground in an ungraceful heap.

Landing hard in the dirt, Arman had the wind knocked out of him. He was working to catch his breath when the person who'd grabbed on to him in the first place started to laugh. They crouched beside him and pulled him up to sitting. Arman blinked and stared, his eyes adjusting to the darkness. Jesus. It was *Kira*.

Beautiful Kira.

She was still laughing. "Hey, kid."

"Hey," he said, pressing his hand to his lungs. "That *hurt*."

"Maybe you want to try not falling on your ass next time." Kira leaned forward, so close that her soft braids brushed against Arman's cheek, causing his heart to leap, among other things. She'd never touched him before. Not on purpose, and he waited, eagerly. Maybe she was going to kiss him—stranger things had happened today—only she didn't. Instead she reached to brush the dirt and leaves from his hair. And she did it vigorously, like he was some ragged pup too filthy to come inside. Like *she* wasn't the one who'd put the dirt there in the first place.

He ducked away. Kira was more hyper than he'd realized. "Stop it."

She grinned a wide Cheshire grin. "Fine."

"Where've you been? Why weren't you at dinner?"

"I *was* at dinner. I saw you sleeping in there, by the way."

Arman scowled. "Well, where's Dale?"

She shrugged.

"Kira . . ."

"Where were *you* this afternoon?" she asked, and under the light of the moon, her eyes were bright, glittering. "You ever going to tell me about that?"

Arman bit his lip. She meant when he'd gone off with Beau. Of course he couldn't tell her about *that*.

Kira grinned wider, crawling to her feet. She reached her hand down to help him up. "See? We both have our secrets. Things we aren't willing to tell."

Arman let her pull him to standing. Kira wrapped her arm through his, an act of closeness that melted his irritation if not his injury. They began to walk, and Arman absorbed the thrum of her energy. He didn't push the secret issue with her because his stomach was hurting, a tight, crampy pain he knew well and deeply resented. Why had he eaten so much? And drank that tea with milk in it? Just thinking about the meal now made him feel gross, swollen and queasy, like a fattened lamb.

That's when Arman lifted his head and stared up the hill toward the dome building.

At the open doors.

At the wood smoke puffing from the chimney.

"Hey, Kira," he said.

"Hey, Arman," she replied.

"What do you think about all this? What do you really think's going to happen here?"

"We're going to learn to make our own lives. Determine our own fate. Isn't that the point?"

"Yeah, but isn't that something you were already doing? I mean, back home, you've always seemed, I don't know . . ."

"I seemed what?"

"Lucky," he said.

She cocked her head. "That's a funny word."

"I didn't mean—"

"No, I know what you *meant*. It's just . . . well, you know who my dad is, right?"

"Sure." Of course he did. Everyone knew. Kira's father was one of the most famous civil-rights attorneys in the state. Maybe even the country.

"Yeah, well, he's pretty used to having people do the things he tells them to. And Dale's one of the things he told me not to do."

"Oh," Arman said. Then: "Because he's white?"

"Because he's *nineteen*. Also he didn't finish high school."

"So you think Dale's worth running away for?"

"I'm not running *away*, kid. I'm here to find myself. To find out how to be better than myself. Aren't you?"

He didn't answer. They were almost at the domed building. Kira was practically skipping, but for Arman, the closer they got to the entrance and the glowing light and the crowds of people all hustling to get inside for a ritual he longed to be a part of but didn't understand, the sicker his stomach felt. He didn't like uncertainty, he realized. Hell, he didn't even like attention.

You like Beau, though. And you can do this. Be who you want to be. For once in your damn life.

So Arman squared his shoulders and set his jaw. Tried to stand up straight, despite the cramping in his gut. This was what he was here for, after all.

To change.

To *evolve*.

"You look nervous," Kira whispered as they approached the threshold.

"I am nervous," Arman whispered back. "I feel like a lamb being led to the slaughter."

She laughed. "You're funny."

"Really?"

She nodded. "You remember that thing Lord Summerisle says at the end of *The Wicker Man*?"

Arman shook his head. He had no idea what she was talking about. "That's a movie, right? I never saw it. What does he say?"

Kira grinned her Cheshire grin again. "'Reverence the sacrifice.'"

Arman wasn't sure what he expected to find inside the meeting hall. Something churchlike, perhaps. Something sacrificial and reverent. Like a space filled with pews and a pulpit. Or maybe something resembling the auditorium at his school—humble in its simplicity—a round room with a stage surrounded by folding chairs and ugly fluorescent lighting. Or hell, maybe they'd just sit on the floor with their legs crossed while Beau stood before them and talked. That'd be fine with him, Arman thought. It was Beau he'd come for.

Nothing else.

But when he and Kira walked inside, no one was sitting anywhere. Instead the place was jammed wall to wall with people standing in small groups and clusters. They laughed and talked and milled about, like it was the easiest thing to do. Like this was a cocktail party. Or a fun night out. Or anything but what it was.

But what was it?

Kira took Arman's hand and pulled him through the crowd. Winding through strangers, with everyone so tightly packed, the panic creep of closeness came over him. It knotted his throat and watered his eyes. Made him feel light-headed. Music was playing, something upbeat with a swing to it, but Arman didn't know where she was leading him. He squeezed her hand and tugged, wanting her to slow down, but she tugged back harder, pulling him deeper into the throng. Arman held on, feet lurching forward in the proper way, but he let his head fall back. Let himself stare at the ceiling. The dome roof was vaulted, towering skyward, and built by interlocking wood beams, an intricate cribbing that formed a dizzying geometric pattern. Between the beams was negative space, open to the outside. Moonlight and cool air drifted down from the heavens.

"Kira," Arman tried to say, but his voice couldn't be heard over the crowd. They moved deeper into the hall. His shoulders and hips bumped against strangers. His forehead grew wet. He was trapped, he realized, in a crush of friendly humanity. He couldn't escape if he wanted to.

Kira, on the other hand, was clearly in her social element. She greeted people with an openness Arman couldn't help but envy. She made it look easy, being among strangers and being noticed; she waved and hugged and spoke with people she hardly knew.

Snippets of conversations swirled around Arman's head as they cut across the room. He couldn't catch everything he heard, but what he did sounded weird, unnervingly so—bizarre stories about past lives and encounter groups and strange somatic practices like craniosacral massage and some sort of energy transfer that required knowledge of auras. Arman was baffled. Living in Santa Cruz, he was used to a lot of fringe types and their New Age ideals, but that wasn't the kind of stuff Beau was into.

Was it?

Finally they reached the dome's center. Here, a stone fireplace roared with flames, sending plumes of smoke up a narrow chimney that vented through the very top of the structure. The fire's heat warmed Arman's legs, his chest.

He looked at Kira.

"I don't feel so good," he said.

"Shhh." She let go of his hand and put a finger to her lips. Arman opened his mouth to say more, like how he might faint, right here in front of everybody, and how that would embarrass him, so maybe he should go do his wilting outside, be separate, be the way he always was. But he realized the whole room had fallen silent. Everyone was turned toward a side entrance, on the opposite side of where they'd come in. Arman turned, too.

It was Beau. He was here.

He stood on a chair in order to be seen.

"Hello," he called to the crowd, and when the murmurs of return greeting died out, he said, "Nice night, isn't it? Why don't we go for a walk?"

Trudging back outside into the cool breeze and heavy blackness of night, Arman felt sicker. Sick enough that he fantasized about slipping away to find a bathroom or a secluded spot in the woods where he could bend over, stick his fingers down his throat, and be done with all the food that churned inside of him. Be done with whatever was making him feel so awful.

It was actually something Arman was doing semi-regularly of late—the making-himself-puke thing. It wasn't a good habit, obviously, but he only did it because he got so many stomachaches, not because he wanted to be skinny or anything. He restrained himself, though, because people were watching and also, it would be a waste of good Adderall. He had a limited supply.

The entire group made their way down into the dark meadow. They hiked along a narrow path that cut through the long grass, then headed up toward the north side of the compound, winding into the dark forest. On all sides, the towering trees drew in close. Then closer. There were no lights here, and Arman kept his sense of time and space by following the shuffling feet of the people in front of him. That was probably how they were moving, too, as well as those who came behind him. It was interesting, he thought, the way a mass of individuals could move as one. Without even meaning to. Maybe that's what the term *hive mind* really meant: not a single consciousness split among many, but rather, a bunch of small parts doing their small bits until the accumulation of those bits worked to create a whole.

They kept walking. Farther and farther. Until Arman's legs hurt along with his stomach. Until his heart felt sore and rattled, unused to so much exertion. Where were they going? What would happen when they got there? The trail stretched on and on, leading them up, up, up toward the starlit sky.

Kira stayed close to Arman as they hiked, although she wasn't touching him anymore. She walked alongside him without saying a word. Every so often, he caught her twisting her head over her shoulder to glance into the darkness behind her. Arman was curious about who or what she was looking for. Maybe like his fear of his stepfather, she was picturing her overprotective father hunting her down. Dragging her home. But before he could open his mouth to ask, the answer appeared. Like an apparition.

Or a wish fulfilled.

"Hey," Dale said easily, stepping out of the night gloom to fall in line beside them. He had jeans on now, not shorts, but other than that, with his red eyes and foot-dragging stride, he looked exactly as Arman remembered.

Kira made a noise of contentment at the sight of him. She wrapped her arms around his waist.

Arman couldn't help himself. He stared at Dale as they walked.

"What is it?" Dale asked.

"Where'd you come from?"

"Back there."

"Well, where've you been? You weren't at dinner."

Dale shrugged. "Nowhere, man."

"You had to be somewhere."

"Just needed some time to myself. That's it."

Arman frowned. When he put it like that, maybe Dale's disappearance really wasn't all that weird. No one had said anything about meals or activities being mandatory, so why did Arman assume they were? Maybe it was his *assumptions* that made him feel like Dale was doing something secretive and bad, not Dale's actions. What was it that short guy at dinner had said to him?

We make our own stories here.

It stood to reason that went for expectations and assumptions, too.

Didn't it?

"Well, why are you here now?" Arman asked.

"Quarantine. Didn't want to miss it."

"Wait. You know about Quarantine? Is that what we're doing next?"

"Next?" Dale stared at him. "Dude. It's what we're doing *now*."

"Huh?"

Dale pointed. The group had reached its destination, it seemed, the whole hive mind mass coming to a stop in a wide clearing that sat at the base of a giant moonlit boulder. Arman tipped his head back and gaped. The rock was *massive*. At least fifty feet high.

"What *is* that?" Arman breathed.

"That's Echo Rock," said Dale.

7

ECHO ROCK INDEED.

A man who wasn't Beau positioned himself at the front of the group. Held his hand up for silence. To Arman, this guy looked like a gym teacher, with a beer gut and a carefully trimmed beard. He also didn't wear any of the gauzy clothes Arman had come to associate with people working at the compound. Instead, he had on rugged jeans and hiking boots, and he asked for everyone who was new to the community that day to come forward.

Arman hesitated. He was pretty sure that meant him but didn't want to be wrong. Not with everyone watching. However, when he saw all the people who'd been in the van with him earlier walk up to the front, he quickly followed.

"You'll be coming with me," the man told them. "And when we get to where it is we're going, I'm going to need you to do exactly as I say. Without question and without hesitation. Do you understand?"

Arman nodded. He intended to follow all the rules. Of course he did. But the person standing next to him gave a loud snort of derision.

Everyone turned to look.

It was Dale.

Stupid Dale.

Before the man in hiking boots could say a word or respond, the crowd parted, like a curtain pulled back, to reveal Beau as he strode to the front of the group, hands clasped before him. When he got there, he turned and stood calmly, the silvery wash of moonlight striping his face. One by one he contemplated the new arrivals.

"Tonight marks the beginning of Quarantine," he began. "An initiation, of sorts, but an unusual one. This is not a test of your worth to bring you into our fold. This is not an act of humiliation meant to make you crave our approval. Quarantine is a chance for *you* to accept us. For you to open your mind as wide as the earth and as deep as the sea, to take in all that we have to offer and to receive our gifts."

Arman tried peeking at Dale to see his expression, if he was open to anything, but it was too dark.

Beau continued, the cadence of his words far more soothing than their content, "Now, I know that none of you know where you're going, but you're going to find yourself there, nonetheless. That's the beauty of Quarantine. It's the beauty of Evolution. But for this initial part of the process, you should also know that *listening* will be your most important skill. In fact"—his lips twitched—"your very life depends on it."

They headed into the trees and left the rest of the group behind. Arman figured he was screwed. Listening had never been his strong suit, no matter how hard he tried. He lagged at the back of the hikers, but from what he could tell they were no longer following any actual trail, just tromping through brush and scrambling over mossy boulders, making their way around the back of Echo Rock. The peak reared above them, a declaration of sorts. Stretching toward the heavens.

Blocking the stars.

Arman felt dizzy again. Where were they going? What would they do when they got there? He couldn't imagine.

But maybe that was the point.

"We're here," the man in front called out, after a few more minutes of trudging through darkness. They'd risen above the tree line and stood backed against the sheer cliff wall, exposed to the wind gusting off the ocean and into the mountains.

"Oh, shit," breathed Dale. "You've got to be shitting me. There's no way. No fucking way."

Well, that didn't sound good. Arman put a hand to his brow. Strained to see what it was that was so disturbing. It took a moment, but he found it: A set of climbing ropes dangled from the top of Echo Rock down to where they stood. The man with the hiking boots had bent down and was beginning to pass out harnesses and climbing helmets. It was pretty clear what they would be asked to do.

Or told, really.

Dale's normally sleepy eyes were the size of Frisbees. "They can't seriously expect us to do *that*. To climb up there. I mean, they can't. It's not safe. It just isn't."

"I don't think it's all *that* far." Arman gazed upward. He'd climbed the rock wall at the Y before and from what he could tell, this distance wasn't much higher than that. Of course, this wall also wasn't inside or well lit and had no pads below. But it had to be safe or they wouldn't be doing it.

Right?

"Shhh!" Kira put a finger to her lips. "I'm trying to listen."

The man began his lecture on safety precautions and how to make the climb. Arman did his best to absorb the information. He wasn't afraid of heights, not like Dale, but he definitely understood what Beau meant about listening now. His life *did* depend on it.

All of theirs did.

The first person to make the ascent was an older woman who had the misfortune of having worn flip-flops. In a way that was good since Arman figured if she could make the climb, he could, too. But he held his breath watching her navigate the rock face. She slipped a few times, her shoes unable to grip the footholds, but the man with the hiking boots coached her from the ground. Persuaded her to keep going.

Dale whirled to face Arman. "What do you think we'll have to do when we get up there?"

"I don't know," Arman said.

"You don't think there's a zip line, do you? Please tell me there's no zip line."

"I don't think there's a zip line."

Dale snapped, "You don't know that!"

Arman scowled, but didn't answer. Whatever. There was no reasoning with fear. And besides, shouldn't Kira be the one trying to reason with him? She was his girlfriend, after all. Only Kira wasn't anywhere near them anymore. She'd pushed her way toward the front of the line.

The first woman made it to the top safely, signaled by a tug on the rope. They couldn't see her at all in the darkness, but the man in the hiking boots waved Kira forward. She clipped in, listened to last-minute instructions, and started to shimmy her way toward the top.

As the remaining members of the group dwindled, Dale began blowing air through his fists.

"I can't do this," he whined. "What do you think'll happen if I don't do it?"

"They might send you home," Arman offered.

"That's it?"

"Come on, you don't want that."

"What I *want* is to not die."

Arman sighed. "You know what my dad used to tell me about fear?"

"What's that?"

"'You only fear what you believe will kill you, never what will.'"

Dale stared at him. Then: "Your dad sounds like a dick."

Arman shrugged.

The man in the hiking boots snapped his fingers. Called Dale's name. Arman expected a huge scene or a full-blown panic attack, but to his surprise Dale threw his shoulders back and walked forward. He grabbed his harness and began to step into it.

"Let's get this shit over with," he muttered. "I'll probably be in therapy for the rest of my life."

"Wait. So you're going to do it? You're actually going to do it?"

Dale gave Arman a shaky thumbs-up.

"But why? What changed your mind?"

Dale threw his hands in the air. "Jesus, man. Why do you think? You just said it's not going to kill me!"

Arman couldn't argue with that. If there was one thing he knew, it was the power of magical thinking. So it was with a tingle of pride that he watched Dale make the climb, slowly but surely, and when it was finally his turn, the last to go, he looked at the man holding the belay rope and gave a shy smile.

"Kind of cool that I was able to help him," he said, pulling on his helmet. Fiddling with the strap.

"Sure," the man said.

"So what do I do when I get up there?"

"You'll know."

"I will?"

"I just said you would."

"Too bad there's not an easier way up."

"Oh, there is." The man gestured eastward. "There's a trailhead about a quarter mile on. It's steep, but walkable."

Arman was confused. "Well, why aren't we using that?"

"Why do you think?"

"Because it's scarier this way?"

"Because always taking the easy route means forgetting there could be others. Maybe better ones. You can't know unless you try."

Pride, it turned out, was a fleeting emotion.

This was the reality Arman faced as he stood perched atop a giant boulder on the very edge of Echo Rock. He hovered high above the clearing where the entire rest of the group—Beau included—stared up at him, and far beneath the soft moon that hung like a beacon in the velvety sky.

Illuminating his failure.

Whatever goodness he'd felt after helping Dale was gone. Long gone. And Arman understood what he was *supposed* to be doing, now that he was here and it was his turn. Now that the other climbers had left, already following the eastern trail back down to the clearing in one big group. They were the ones, as Arman had crawled, gasping, over the final precipice and unbuckled himself from his harness and helmet, who'd told him where to go and what to do.

Only they hadn't told him *how*.

So he did nothing but stand there.

He watched the wind rattle the trees below.

He watched the needles fall from the branches.

State your truth, they'd told him. *State it loud.* And why was that so hard? Why would it be easier for him to run and hide or claw his skin or simply swan dive to his death rather than do what was being asked of him?

His knees trembled, but he kept standing there. Right on the edge.

But Arman also kept *thinking*. Of what he'd left behind. Of what he'd found in the short time he'd been here.

Like the cook's affection.

Like Mari's kindness.

Like Beau's blind faith in him.

And he thought of the people below. Surely they already knew the truth about how pathetic he was. Standing up here for so long, it wasn't something he could hide.

So it doesn't matter what you say, he told himself. *Speak or don't speak. No one's listening anyway.*

That's when Arman took a deep breath and leaned forward. He cupped his hands around his mouth and then he shouted out the words he didn't want to admit, but which lived and breathed in the rawest parts of his being.

A moment later, on the wide wings of the dark night wind, a hundred echoing voices from the clearing below rushed Arman's truth right back at him.

"*I don't belong here!*" they cried. "*I don't think I can change!*"

DOING YOUR BEST.

There's an unfair assumption, you feel. That by design you don't believe the things you say. That your every word, every deed, is meant as magic. As misdirection. From this follows the notion that what is calculating and deliberate must also be false. That if something is true, it must be obvious, and therefore easy.

But the truth is never easy. Your own father taught you that, in his slick way, with his cool power of persuasion. "Never tell them what they want to hear," he'd whisper. "Tell them what they'll never know."

So what you know is this: The truth is something that can be knotted and dark and rooted so deeply that no one even remembers how it came to be. It can be utterly painful. It can be unspeakably cruel.

It can also be very hard to swallow.

That's where you come in, all sweet talk and honeyed tones. You have the power to make the truth taste richer than the kindest lie. You don't lure the innocent into darkness so much as you open their eyes to the vast night sky. That is your gift.

The only lies are the ones you tell yourself.

That you're a good person.

That you're doing what's best.

8

AND THEN THERE WAS LIGHT.

Lots of it.

Arman stared down from the edge of Echo Rock. He was awestruck not only by what he'd done, but what he saw. Nearly every single person below had brought with them some object of illumination—hidden from sight before but now out in the open— flashlights, lanterns, headlamps, even those glowing sticks children wore around their necks on Halloween. There were candles, too, scores of them—long tapers threaded through Dixie-cup bases, flickering votives held inside Mason jars, even thick pillars gripped in gloved hands—all lit so quickly it was as if a switch had been flipped. The whole clearing, dark one moment, was now brilliantly aglow. Tiny earthly stars danced in every dimension: their warm light bouncing off granite, shooting up into the trees.

Arman's heart swelled.

It was just so *beautiful.*

The night breeze ruffled his hair, his skin tingled with rare plea- sure, and Arman didn't want to move. He didn't want to leave this moment. He didn't want to change one damn thing. Yet even in the midst of such beauty and awe, he could still feel the telltale scrabble of rising panic. Was *he* supposed to have brought something? Was he meant to have a light of his own? Maybe his small part was what was missing from this breathtaking whole. Maybe he was screwing up a responsibility he didn't even know was his.

Shit.

With newfound worry came familiar guilt, and Arman fled the rock. He found the trailhead and scrambled back down to the clearing, carefully navigating the steep terrain so as not to fall to his death. Landing on the forest floor, however, he had no time for questions; he was greeted too quickly by joyous faces and kind words and outstretched hands that clapped his back and squeezed his shoulders and told him how *brave* he'd been. Arman did his best to stand tall in the face of such praise and admiration. These were things he definitely wasn't used to and probably never would be. Hell, he'd only done what had been asked of him on Echo Rock because he was too scared not to. It's not like that was *real* bravery.

Was it?

Then Beau was there. He emerged like a vision from the sea of strangers to throw an arm around Arman, to give him a hale pat and a hearty hug, and in the wake of his presence, Arman couldn't help but feel good. Well, better, at least. Less frantic. More in control.

"Wonderful job up there, Arman. Really wonderful." Beau grinned, and the light he held in his hand was the brightest of all: an old camping lantern, one powered not by batteries but by kerosene, its fat wick brazen with greasy flame-heat. "I knew you could do it. Now you know, too."

"Thank you." Arman squirmed. He hated to sound boastful but didn't know what else to say.

"You ready for the walk back?" Beau asked.

"I think so. But do I need my own light? I didn't bring one."

"Of course you don't need your own light," Beau said. "You have ours."

It took Arman a moment to realize what was happening. Actually, it took him a moment to realize anything was happening at all.

Without a word, a group of maybe a dozen or so flashlight and candle and lantern holders—Beau included—slowly separated themselves from the crowd and began to surround Arman. In a deliberate sort of way. They moved in unison and linked their arms. They wrapped themselves around him and closed their human circle in tight, then tighter, until he was the sole point of darkness in the center of their light.

Once formed, the circle began to move. Slow, deliberate steps. Like a walking wave. Their momentum pushed Arman along with them, herding him away from the clearing, back onto the trail.

Arman hopped on his toes and looked around. He wasn't the only one being separated from the group. Kira and Dale were also being corralled into their own glowing circles, along with all the other people who'd braved the climb to the top of Echo Rock and confessed their most-intimate truths. Each and every one of them was being swallowed up and subsumed into a ring of luminescence. A symbol of protection, perhaps. Or containment. Arman wasn't sure which word best described the act of Quarantine.

Either way, he moved as he was meant to. He had no choice in the matter. While the group surrounding him was determined in their silence, it was clear that this was how they were going to hike back down the mountain—with them herding and him obeying.

Arman didn't think he much liked this turn of events. Not one bit.

But you can do it, he told himself, and that's what propelled him forward. This was just another test. Another way to prove his strength. And while Arman didn't care for tests or any evaluation of his merit, he understood the pragmatism of it all. Otherwise how would anyone know what he was capable of?

Least of all, himself.

9

"TELL US WHY YOU DON'T belong."

The words hung in the cool night air. Startled, Arman glanced over at the woman on his left who'd spoken them. She wasn't anyone he recognized, but she was one of the people gripping a thin candle sleeved by a Dixie cup meant to catch any dripping wax. She held the candle low, by her waist, so that her face was hidden in shadows.

That's when Arman realized the woman was speaking to *him*.

"Wait, what?" he asked.

"On Echo Rock. You said you don't belong here. Tell us why."

Us? Arman looked around. Saw pairs of eyes watching him closely. Not Beau's, though. The circle had shifted somewhat—their arms now unlinked—but Beau still walked at the front. Always the leader. Arman could only make out his back. His square shoulders.

Those strange flowy clothes.

"Why, I don't know why," said Arman.

"Sure you do," called another voice. "You said it, didn't you?"

"Tell us," insisted a third. This from a man on Arman's right.

Arman blinked. "I really *don't* know. That's the truth. I guess—I guess I just feel like anytime there's the potential for something good in my life,

I fuck it up. So I don't belong anywhere. Not anywhere I want to be."

"Tell us what you fuck up," the man said, and there was something in his tone that felt like an affirmation of Arman's guilt. Of his inevitable fucked-up-ed-ness.

"*Everything*," he said. "My family. My social life. The basketball team I went out for in eighth grade. A church group I tried joining in tenth. Even coming here. I mean, all I ever want is to feel a part of something. Instead I'm always the piece that doesn't fit."

"How'd you fuck up your family?" another voice asked, but Arman couldn't see who it was.

"I fucked up by being born," he mumbled.

"Bullshit!" someone behind him called out.

"No self-pity," shouted another. "Everyone your age says that. You're not special."

"Be honest," the first woman told him firmly. The one with the low, drippy candle.

Arman's throat went dry. Was there a point to all this? Was he supposed to feel like he was on the verge of passing out or throwing up on his shoes? If that was the case, well, then things were going just great. And he wasn't *lying*. His birth was the unfortunate glue that had kept his parents together long after they should have been apart. Those were the years that broke his mother; left her estranged from her family and more bitter than ever when the inevitable split did come. "Fine. For starters, my mom doesn't like me. She divorced my dad when I was nine and got remarried to a guy who hates my guts. He treats her like crap. In return she treats me pretty crappy, and honestly, I do the same to her."

"That's it?" the woman asked.

"I don't know. I'm kind of moody. And I'm anxious a lot."

"So your being *anxious* fucks things up?"

Arman's head grazed a tree branch as he walked, dumping a flurry of dead leaves into his hair. "No. I mean, it's not just being anxious. It's my whole brain. Who I am. I can't do things sometimes. I get overwhelmed. So I don't do anything. It's gotten me in trouble since I was a kid. My mom's had to deal with that, I guess."

"How'd she deal with it?"

"Took me to a doctor." Arman held a hand in front of his face. He didn't want to run into anything else he couldn't see.

"What'd the doctor do?" she asked.

"Put me on medication."

"And now you don't get overwhelmed anymore?"

"No, I still do."

"Then what's the point of the medication?"

"The point is that I don't get in trouble as much. I can focus. I can finish things that I start."

"So you take pills, not to feel better, but to finish things that you start and to stay out of trouble?"

"I guess." Arman squinted into the darkness ahead. "Are we almost back now? My legs hurt. I'm tired."

"Jesus," someone behind him muttered. "What's with this kid?"

"How's school for you then?" the woman asked. "Is it better? Now that you're on medication?"

Arman snorted. "*No.* I hate school."

"What do you hate about it?"

Was there something *not* to hate? "It sucks. People don't like me. And I don't mean they *dislike* me either. They just don't notice me. Do you know how many times someone's turned off the classroom lights while I'm still in the room? Students. Teachers. It doesn't matter. They don't see me." *I'm a ghost*, he longed to add but didn't. Even he knew how pathetic it would sound.

"Are you only worth what other people see in you?" the woman asked.

"Yeah. Sure. How people value you determines how they treat you, right? Well, people treat me like I'm invisible. And you know what? Maybe I am."

"How do you treat yourself?"

"The way I deserve to be treated."

"Where's your dad, Arman? Your real dad?"

"Nowhere good."

"What does that mean?"

"It means he's in prison at the moment. He'll be there for a while."

"Why's he in prison?"

"Uh-uh," Arman said, and one of his legs was really hurting now. The left one. He'd banged it climbing up that rock. "No way. I'm not going to talk about my father. He's not important."

"Why are you bleeding?"

A surprise: It was *Beau* who'd asked this question. He'd even turned around to do it, and unlike the rest of the group, he held his lantern up to his face as he spoke, showing the warmth of his expression. The wisdom in his eyes. For a flash of an instant, Arman met his gaze.

Then he looked down.

Fuck. He'd scratched open the scab on his arm. Not only that, but he'd dug deeper into the wound. Without even realizing it. Blood dripped freely down his wrist. Arman yanked his shirtsleeve down and pressed hard on the gash. Tried to get it to stop.

"Why are you bleeding?" Beau asked again.

"I don't *know*," Arman snapped. "I just am."

No one responded to this. Not verbally, at least. But the group stopped walking, their glowing lights coming to a sudden halt. This meant Arman had to stop, too. He stood in the center of all those watching eyes. Kept pressing at his arm.

"What's going on?" he asked. "Why aren't we going anywhere?"

Still nothing.

"Hello?"

One by one the people around him sat in the dirt. They held their candles and flashlights and lanterns beneath their chins, so that the lower halves of their faces were visible. It was like watching the tide roll out from the beach to expose the glittering life below, but it was what *didn't* come into view that made Arman's heart stutter. He didn't see any of the other groups. There were no bobbing lights in the distance. No Kira. No Dale. Worse, he didn't even recognize where he was, didn't remember passing through this grove of eucalyptus trees or walking along the edge of this fog-filled ravine.

Arman wiped his nose with his sleeve. Glanced back at the people surrounding him. Their wall of watchful eyes and flickering candles felt less like protection and more like he was about to be burned at the stake.

"Fine," he said flatly. "I made myself bleed. Is that what you want to know? It's something I do when I get stressed. I can't help it."

"Why are you stressed?" Beau asked.

"Because of *this* . . . what we're doing right now. I don't want to bare my soul to strangers. That's a shitty thing to have to do. For me, at least. That's not why I'm here."

"Then why are you here?"

"You don't know?"

"How can I know unless you tell me?"

Arman made a gasping sound. He clawed at his throat, digging his nails as deep as they would go. "I'm here to make you proud of me!"

"Me?"

"Yes!"

There was another beat of silence. Then: "Sit down, Arman."

He shook his head. "No. I want to go back. I'm sorry. I don't want to do this."

"Sit," Beau commanded.

So he sat. Right in the damn dirt.

Beau leaned forward. Took both of Arman's hands in his. The kerosene lantern burned bright between them, and Beau held on to him for what seemed like forever.

He held.

And held.

And held.

"I can feel your pain," Beau said at last. "It's hot. Like a fever. Your sickness runs deep, son. No wonder you're willing to spill your own blood to get rid of it."

Arman stared at the ground. "Whatever."

"Do you understand that I want to help you?"

"Yeah. I guess."

"Then you have to trust me."

"I *do*. It's just—"

"And you have to help me in return."

"But how can I do that? I don't know what I'm supposed to do. I don't know anything!"

"Stand with me." Beau got to his feet. Arman got up with him but staggered, woozy, as spots flashed before his eyes.

"I'm fine," he said, but Beau grabbed on to him. Held him steady. Then he pushed Arman's shirtsleeves up. Exposed his bleeding wound and all the scars of wounds long past.

"You have to stop hurting yourself," Beau said softly.

"I *know.*"

"I mean it. You've been taught to turn your pain inward. But that's wrong. It's sick. Do you understand me?"

Arman nodded. "I . . . I think so."

"*No!*" Beau hissed. "That's your whole damn problem, *thinking.* Ever since the day we met, you've told me what you *think* about things. But you don't *feel* and you don't *do.* Not in any meaningful way. Feeling and doing, they're more important than the thoughts inside your head. They're our primary channels to health. To *immunity.*"

"Huh?" Arman shivered. He couldn't even pretend to comprehend what was going on.

Beau sighed. "Do you take care of yourself by thinking about exercising? Or by actually exercising?"

"Actually exercising."

"And does thinking about, say, sex keep you from wanting it? Or do you find you're driven to satisfy your desires in more physical ways?"

At this, a great roar of laughter rose up behind him, and Arman longed to melt. Or evaporate. Did everyone know about him and the cook? That's what it felt like. But he managed to answer, "I . . . satisfy my desires."

"I would hope so," Beau said smoothly. "So when I say that you need to express your pain externally, what is it that you need to do?"

"I need to do it."

"That's right." A look of approval crossed Beau's face, and seeing this calmed Arman. It reassured him that he was saying the right things and doing what was expected of him. It also gave him hope this ordeal would soon be over. He watched eagerly as Beau rolled his own shirtsleeves up, exposing the smooth skin of his forearms. Then Beau pulled something from the side pocket of his pants. He worked hard to pry whatever it was open before dropping it right in the center of Arman's palm.

Gasps came from the surrounding circle, and Arman stared, disbelieving. It was a knife. Beau had given him a pocketknife. A strange-looking one, with a rosewood handle and an ornate type of blade Arman had never seen before. Rather than a solid steel color, this blade was a dramatic mix of light and dark, of everything in between. Streaks of grays and blacks covered the entire surface—a gleaming feat of metallurgy that worked to form a distinctive pattern of whorls and loops. Like a fingerprint.

"My grandfather made it," Beau said. "It's a Damascus. Truly one of a kind."

Arman said nothing. He just kept staring at the blade.

Then he looked at Beau's outstretched, unscarred arms. Like an offering.

A sacrifice.

For *him*.

"Wait a minute," Arman said slowly, shaking his head. "No. No, I won't do that. Of course not. I won't hurt you."

"Yes, you will. You'll do it now. Go on."

Arman swallowed hard. His trembling hand closed around the knife's hilt. It was heavier than he'd realized, and it was nothing for him to let the weight of the decorative blade tip down to rest against Beau's soft wrist. He glanced up.

"I can't do this," he said.

"You can. You will."

Arman nodded. Held his breath. Then he began pressing down on the blade. Slowly. Very slowly. Until *pop!* The skin gave. A dot of red appeared. The smallest mark. He quickly looked at Beau again. He wanted approval. He wanted to be told to stop.

"Deeper." Beau fixed his calm river-pebble gaze on him. "As deep as you can go. To the *bone.*"

"What?" Arman yanked his hand back. "No!"

"You said you wanted to heal."

"Yeah, but not like this. This isn't healing. It's gross."

"Are you sure, Arman? Or is that just what you think?"

Was this really happening? "I'm sure I think it's *true.*"

Beau bent forward then, lowering his voice to a whisper, making it a moment just between them. "Maybe the truth is that you don't know what healing looks like. Maybe nothing you know is as it seems."

"And why would that be?"

"Because you're *here.* Because you can't see the truth from where you're standing. Because you're like a dog chasing a squirrel as it runs around a tree. You don't realize you could catch the damn thing if you just stood still."

Thick and heavy, Arman's nausea had returned to roost. "So what? I'm just supposed to do something I don't want to do because you think I should?"

"*Alia tentanda via est.* That's our motto here."

"I don't even know what that *means!*"

"It means 'another way must be tried.'"

Of course it did. And of course Arman understood. This was the moment he was meant to crack. This was the moment that he was meant to see the error of his ways and demonstrate that his disgust and self-loathing were far better off directed at the people in his life who'd actually caused him pain.

The thing was Arman *didn't* see it that way. The truth of who he was and why was so much more complicated than that. The swipe of a sword at a self-appointed father figure couldn't begin to bear that burden.

Besides, what Beau was asking him to do, well, it was *wrong*.

It wasn't right.

So Arman gripped the knife, as tight as he could, and with a snarl, he flung the weapon out of the circle. It arced high in the night air, spinning end over end, before tumbling over the edge of the ravine to vanish into the blackness.

"*No*," he told Beau again. "I *won't* do that."

10

FAILURE WAS A MISERABLE THING.

Whether born of courage or conviction, weakness or ineptitude, it never much mattered. Failure wasn't softened by familiarity or tempered by expectation. It wasn't even gilded by good intentions.

It just sucked.

The way it always did.

The rest of the hike back down the mountain was a quiet affair. After Arman's act of petty defiance, the night's magic was broken, and he limped alongside the rest of the group with his head hung low. As before, he had to leach the light of others to keep from falling on his ass or breaking his neck. Only now, instead of a gift, it felt like stealing. Or freeloading.

Or something.

They marched straight for the domed building. Despite the late hour, what came next was a celebration. A grand one. Full of joy and mirth and revelry.

But the party wasn't for Arman.

Of course it wasn't.

It was, however, for everyone else who'd completed the Quarantine stage without shutting down or acting like an asshole. They were on their way to success. They were going to defeat their social order sickness and find happiness. And enlightenment. What greeted *them* when they entered the hall was a warm fire and warm drinks and laughter and dancing and hugs from strangers who were becoming far less strange with every passing hour. No one greeted Arman, though. No one even looked at him.

I'm the strange one, he realized, after settling himself on the floor in a far corner of the room. But he always had been. That was nothing new or revelatory. It was just . . . well, nothing had *changed*. He was still alone and invisible, while across the room Kira, always the popular girl, was still just as popular. Even the two intimidating trainers he'd sat with at dinner—the short man and the dark-haired woman—were talking to her, hanging on her every word with broad smiles on both their faces.

Arman closed his eyes. Let his head fall back against the wall. He tried not to dwell on it, but he didn't understand how he always ended up here. Why he always opted for nothing in the moments when he could have something. Hell, it was only last week that he'd sat at that small café table with a pencil and paper and taken the screening exam Beau had given him.

- Do you ever wake up to find yourself filled with an unexplained feeling of dread?
- Do you experience stomach pains on a regular basis?
- Skin problems?
- Emotional disturbances?
- Are there parts of yourself that you keep suppressed, no matter the cost?

- Do you feel that you could achieve so much more in life if you just knew how?

Yes, Arman had written. *Yes, yes, yes.* Because filling out that paper, for the first time ever in his life, he'd felt understood. Like a hole inside of him he knew was empty suddenly had a reason to be filled. Yet, even then, in the midst of his own awakening, Arman had hesitated. But Beau had seen through that. He'd leaned across the table, glanced at Arman's answers, then looked him in the eye. "I know you think you can't do it," he'd whispered in the same hushed tone he'd used up on the mountain tonight. Only there, in the café, it'd kept Dale and Kira from overhearing his words. It also made Arman feel special. "But that thinking isn't you, son. It's a lie. A lie meant to keep you desperate. See, when you're desperate, you're grateful for what you're given. You don't think you deserve more. But you do, Arman. You deserve so much." And with that it was set. Arman couldn't say no. Not to Beau. He couldn't let down the first person who saw something good in him. Who believed he could be more than he was.

Only now, mere hours after his arrival, Arman was right back where he'd started. With no change in sight.

Maybe that's what he was good at then. Inertia.

Well, there was another thing he was good at, wasn't there?

With that Arman began making plans. The day had been long; the night longer, and when everyone went to sleep, that's when he would slip away. That's when he would take his things and go. He owed no one here anything, and it was clear he wasn't wanted. If Beau felt like helping another charity case or if he just wanted a partner to help stop whoever wanted to ruin this community for him, he'd do better picking just about anyone else. Dale, included. And with the money he had, Arman figured he could go anywhere. Be anyone. Sort of.

A list of faraway cities cartwheeled through his mind. Intriguing places he'd seen on TV or watched in movies. Los Angeles. Denver. Seattle. Santa Fe. He could get a job. Rent a room. Be nobody where no one knew him.

There could be a peace in that, he thought, albeit an imperfect one. But who the hell was he to ask for more?

The party disbanded soon after, but not before Beau stood on a chair again at the front of the room and waved at the crowd amidst rousing applause. He praised everyone for their participation. For their vulnerability and courage. Quarantine had been a sterling success, he said, and not merely as a ritual. No, there was nothing symbolic about the work they'd done. By facing their fears and bringing the source of their mind's disease to the surface, they were now poised to do battle. And win.

Arman's sense of shame flared hotter, higher. He'd battled nothing, of course, and other than that fleeting spark of joy up on Echo Rock, this whole night, everything he'd done, had been a waste.

Beau had two final instructions for the group. "The first," he implored, "is a commitment from you not to speak with anyone outside of this room about the things we do here or the principles you've learned. Honor the process. Honor yourselves. Do you understand?" There was a murmur of assent. A lot of nodding heads.

"The second is a commitment to not talk about your Before Lives outside of the exercises we'll be doing together. Embrace the chance to be who you are now. The evolution starts with you."

And with that he sent them off to bed.

Is this all bullshit? Arman thought as he slunk into the darkness. *Seriously. Is that what this is?*

Maybe.

But maybe that wasn't the point.

The cabin was deserted when he got there. Arman switched the overhead light on and sat on the edge of his cot. He waited and waited for Kira and Dale to show up. Only they didn't.

Arman poured himself a cup of water from the pitcher that had been left on the table. He drank it slowly, then changed from his jeans and bloodstained shirt into a pair of sweatpants and a T-shirt. After turning off the light, he lay in the dark between the scratchy white sheets, set the alarm on his phone, and shoved it under his pillow.

Two hours. He'd let himself sleep for two hours.

Then he'd be up and out of here.

For good.

EXACT PAYMENT.

Money changes everything. That's the reason people don't like to talk about it. That's the reason they build up walls and proprieties, and insist the topic's rude. Or gauche. Or unprofessional. Maybe you believed that once, too.

Money's the last thing the girl wants to talk about, of course, and you know why. It's too close to the truth. It's too close to acknowledging that anything—and everything—can be bought and sold.

Things like faith.

And honesty.

And trust.

Most of all, trust.

But you talk to her about it in very direct terms. You don't use euphemisms or estimates. You say what you mean. You tell her what you're worth. Money is like sex, you say. It's best with the lights on.

This gets a reaction out of her. It gets her to toss her hair and lift her chin, like she has the upper hand for once. Sex is infinitely better with the lights off, she tells you. Surprises are good, in bed and in life. So is mystery.

But you stand firm. You always do, because you know, without a doubt, that mystery without trust equals fear and the only surprises anyone ever truly wants are the ones they already expect.

The girl argues with you more, a spirited back-and-forth. But ultimately, your resistance is what draws her in.

It's what breaks her down.

It's exactly what makes her pay.

11

THE WORLD WAS STILL DARK when Arman's phone vi-
brated him awake. His eyes flew open, and he sat straight up in the
cabin's grainy blackness. Then groaned. His whole body was stiff
and sore. His shoulders. His back. His knees, especially. They *hurt*.
Even his head throbbed, and while it was hard to believe a single
glass of wine could be the cause, this all-over-everywhere ache was
exactly what he imagined a hangover to feel like.

He shut off the alarm. Peered about the room. He could make out
the motionless forms of Kira and Dale on the other side of the cabin.
They lay huddled beneath a pile of blankets with their arms around
each other. Dale snored softly, while Arman stared at them both.
When had they come back? And where had they been? Maybe there'd
been other events he'd missed, even after the party. Maybe he hadn't been
welcome.

Slipping from cot to floor, Arman took care to land on quiet feet.
No doubt his roommates would be glad to be rid of him, but that didn't
mean he wanted them to know he was leaving. He didn't want to have
to explain *why*.

After feeling around in the bottom of his bag to make sure his stepfather's money was where he'd left it, Arman pulled a gray hooded sweatshirt on over the clothes he was already wearing and put on his shoes. Then, when he was ready, he gathered up the rest of his belongings, slung his messenger bag over one shoulder, and pushed his way out of the cabin.

Once outside, Arman hung close to the tree line as he walked. He was eager to stay in the shadows and not be seen. Although barely four in the morning, a slim gold line already hovered above the eastern mountains. The brass stain of the emerging dawn.

He headed for the iron gate at the entrance to the compound. Even if it was locked, he should be able to scale the fence. Hit the main road. From there he'd head west, traveling until he reached the Pacific Coast Highway. That's where he would catch a ride. Let fate settle the rest. Start life anew.

Again.

"Hey," a soft voice said. "Don't go."

Arman spun around, hackles raised. He was filled with a rare surge of righteousness. He had the freedom to go. He had the freedom to do whatever he wanted.

Didn't he?

But as his eyes adjusted to the hazy darkness, Arman's righteousness faded into shock.

The cook stood on the dirt path with her arms folded, and her legs were no longer bare. She had on black leggings and a gray hooded sweatshirt almost identical to the one Arman wore.

"What are you doing here?" he asked.

She gave him a funny look. "I came to see you."

"Me? Why?"

"I didn't want you to leave."

"How'd you know I was leaving?"

The cook tipped her head to one side. "That's sort of hard to explain."

"Can you try?"

"How about I show you instead?"

"Huh?"

"Come," she whispered, and she turned to head back up the hillside, back into the moonlit meadow where the wind rustled the long grass and the air smelled of loam and stars twinkled overhead like dreams.

Something deep inside Arman whispered, *Don't go, don't follow her* and *Leave while you can.* Only he didn't leave. No, he veered straight off his path toward freedom and followed the cook to a destination unknown. Her hips swayed and her voice lured, and he followed her like a snake to the grass or an early bird after its worm, and wasn't that the weakness of his gender? This single-minded pursuit of warmth and release. The chase of a promise, so brief, so mercurial, yet so utterly, utterly irresistible.

12

TOGETHER THEY WOUND THROUGH GRASS and garden. Dewdrops clung to closed petals and mice scurried in the shadows. An owl screeched overhead, soaring to rub the night sky, and the cook reached for Arman's hand. She led him past the dining hall and the dome and up into the woods, where a small wood-shingled house sat separate, but not far, from the cluster of cabins where Arman had been staying. That must be how she knew he was leaving. From this vantage point, she would've easily seen him walking away.

If she'd been watching for him, that is.

Approaching the house, the cook turned and put a finger to her lips. Arman nodded, but couldn't help wondering who might hear them. They walked through the front door, but before he could look around, she dragged him down a long hallway and shoved him into a room on his left. When they were both inside, the cook shut the door. And locked it.

Arman stood in the center of the room. A small floor lamp lit the space. They were in a bedroom, it seemed, *her* bedroom. Not the cleanest place: All the surfaces were covered in a thick layer of dust and grime, and the cook's clothes lay scattered about, along with a few books and dishes and some personal items, like her hairbrush and her toothbrush and what he thought might be a box of tampons. Clean or not, Arman's heart thrummed to see objects so intimate, to bear witness to these small parts of who she was.

Then he looked at her.

She was already looking back.

"What did you want to show me?" he managed to ask, but his voice came out all croaky and weird.

"Shhh," she told him. "We have to be quiet."

"Sorry," he said quietly.

She smiled.

"Tell me your name," he whispered. "Tell me why we're here."

"You know why," she said.

"I do?"

"Of course." She pulled him closer. "Isn't *that* why you came?"

It was strange, Arman thought after, how *wanting* could be taking a sort of action. For so long, for so many years, he'd imagined that if a beautiful girl ever wanted him, her wanting would be a gift, infusing him with confidence, happiness, a sense of self-esteem. But it wasn't like that. On the contrary, Arman found that the cook's eager wanting took things from him. His focus. His intent. His sense of all rational thought.

But it was worth it.

Hell, it was worth *more*.

"You shouldn't leave," she told him as they lay together in her rumpled sheets, with a hint of gray-gold dawn seeping through the window.

"I have to," he said. "I fucked up last night. I can't stay."

The cook—who still hadn't told him her name and wouldn't—didn't answer. Instead she crawled from the bed, and turned on the hot water kettle she had in the corner of the room. She was still naked, and he could see the stickiness from what they'd done glistening on the inside of her thighs. It made Arman want to do the whole thing all over again. And again after that. Only he didn't know how to ask. He only knew how to answer.

Whistling softly, she made them both tea with honey, keeping the larger mug for herself. Arman sat up and sipped his gratefully. The heat and sweetness felt good, nourishing.

His head felt drowsy.

His limbs tingled with warmth.

The cook settled beside him on the bed. "You didn't fuck up, you know."

"Oh, I did. Trust me."

"No," she insisted. "Beauregard, he sees something in you. He says you're different. Special. He says you have the potential to understand the things he's trying to teach better than anyone he's ever met."

"I don't believe that," Arman said.

"It's true."

"I mean, maybe he thought that before. But last night . . . I was supposed to be part of something, and I didn't do what he wanted me to. I couldn't."

The cook shrugged. "Well, I don't know about that. But I heard him talking after the party last night. He spoke very highly of you."

"*After* the party?"

"Yes."

"That doesn't make sense."

"Sure it makes sense," she said. "You just don't know how."

Arman sighed. "I suppose."

"You're still going to leave, aren't you?"

He nodded.

At this, the cook frowned, then stroked his cheek, an act that made

Arman feel like a child but also made him feel loved. For a moment he thought he might cry, because she was right; he *was* going to leave. It's what he meant to do in the first place, only now it felt less like a choice and more like exile.

So much for freedom.

Arman finished his tea. He relished the warmth in his stomach and the fact that she'd made it for him, and when he'd gotten dressed and was ready to go, he put his hand on the doorknob. Looked back at her. "Can I ask you something?"

"Sure," she said.

"Maybe more than one thing."

"Okay."

"How long have you been here? How long have you known Beau?"

"A long time."

"Then why do you stay? You've been inoculated. You have immunity to, you know, whatever's out there. Whatever's hurt you. You could leave and you'd be fine, right?"

"Immunity isn't just about changing yourself," the cook said. "Not to me. To me it means being a part of something greater, part of a system that helps others change, too. That's what's important. That's everything."

"Everything?"

She nodded. "It fills my needs."

"What are those?"

"To feel capable. Autonomous. Connected to people I care about."

"That's all?"

"What else could there be?"

Arman didn't have an answer for that. "Well, has Beau ever wanted you to do something you felt was wrong? Something you weren't comfortable with?"

"No. Never. But . . ."

"But what?" Arman asked.

The cook smiled. "But I think we have a different sense of morality, you and I. I don't think we're the same at all."

Back outside. There was sunlight now, sweet quicksilver shards of it, piercing the fog and the night and the thick branches of the trees, and seeing as Arman knew full well where the cook was at the moment, he headed straight for the kitchen. He wasn't worried about being seen.

The building was unlocked, as he imagined everything at the compound was, so maybe he wasn't *really* stealing. Maybe everything here was here for the taking. He moved through the room quickly, though, picking a few items to slip into his bag: fruit and bread and raw almonds and bottled water.

When he had what he needed, he hoisted the bag back onto his shoulder. Then he left the kitchen by way of the sliding glass door and walked down to the iron gate. It turned out he didn't have to do any fence climbing when he got there; the heavy chain hung loose, and Arman simply pulled open the right side of the gate. It made a low creaking sound, but that was all. There were no alarms. No gunshots. No one came shouting at him.

Nothing.

Arman slipped out and quietly shut the gate behind him. He glanced over his shoulder only once as he walked away, looking back at those large words that loomed above him like a warning.

"*Alia tentanda via est,*" he whispered. "I'm still trying."

13

DUE WEST. JUST KEEP HEADING west.

You'll get there.

Before setting out, Arman had thought the heading west thing would be a simple enough proposition. And maybe it would've been, if the road leading away from the compound had been anything close to straight or straightforward. Like the world's worst metaphor, the road he was on wound westward through the semi-coastal mountain range like a coiled snake, turning in on itself, again and again, as it crept through valleys and cut across hilltops.

But Arman kept going. He had no other options. His phone, which he'd considered turning off in case his stepfather decided to track him down via GPS, ran out of juice on its own, effectively making the decision for him. So he walked and he walked. Until the sun rose high in the sky and his knee swelled and his hoodie came off and he went back to wishing he were the kind of person who maybe wore shorts every now and then. There was no shade down by the roadside. No ferns or woodsy clearings or burbling creeks. There was nothing but yellow grass. Cracked asphalt.

A soaring heat index.

More time passed. Arman's allergies flared and his head filled with worry—pointless, irrational thoughts, each fretful one landing in his brain like a rock in a water cup to push his anxiety level higher and higher. First, he worried he'd made a wrong turn and gotten lost. Then, he worried he might die of sunstroke. Next, he worried everyone else in the world had been Raptured and he'd be alone for all eternity. Finally, he worried that no one else besides him had ever even existed in the first place.

Wouldn't that be something?

To be fair, none of these scenarios seemed implausible; Arman hadn't seen a single car or house or person the entire time he'd been out here. And now he'd walked for so long, he didn't even think he could make it back to the compound if he wanted to. Which he didn't.

But still.

Then it happened. Without warning, Arman came around a sharp bend in the sloping road and found signs of human life. Right in front of him! It wasn't much, true, but there was a large red barn with the words LOS PADRES MARKET painted in block letters on its roof. There was even a parking lot in the back. He could make out the shadowy shapes of cars that sat in the shade beneath a pair of elm trees.

Maybe, if Arman had been the type to show emotion or wear his heart on his sleeve, the sight of the barn would've gotten him to kick up his heels or whoop with joy. But he wasn't. He simply hurried forward with hope in his veins. He didn't know what he might find inside the market, but there had to be people. If nothing else, he'd at least get a good idea how much farther he had to go. That would ease his mind, he thought, if not his feet, which were starting to blister. But maybe he could get a ride from someone. Maybe luck would be on his side.

For once.

————

Arman pushed open the market door and stepped inside. A bell jangled overhead. He was smacked in the face by air-conditioner chill and the smell of burnt pizza. But the assault felt good: sweet relief from the day's heat.

There were no people he could see. Rows of packaged foods and various sundries stretched before him. An ice machine stood against the far wall, and on Arman's right, a long ramp led down to a second room, one filled with empty tables and chairs. A huge television was mounted to the wall. He ducked to see what was on. It was baseball. Stupid Giants.

People or no people, Band-Aids were a high priority for Arman at the moment. He cruised the grocery aisles until he found them wedged between a can of jock itch spray and medicine meant to stop diarrhea and heartburn. Arman wasn't sure how Band-Aids might be used to bridge that gap, but whatever. He grabbed the first box he saw.

"Nice pants," a voice said.

"Huh?" Arman looked up. A teenage boy about his age stood at the very end of the aisle. He was tall with a long nose, short black hair, and he wore a blue apron with the message "Welcome to the Los Padres Market. How May I Help You Today?" printed on the front. "What did you say about my pants?"

"Looks like you pissed yourself."

"It's *sweat*," Arman said. "They're sweatpants. It's hot out there, you know."

The boy smirked. "Whatever you say. Where you going anyway? You walked here. No one walks here."

"I'm trying to get to the highway."

"Which highway?"

Were there others? "The PCH."

"Dude, you got like twelve miles to go."

Arman gaped. "You serious?"

"Dead serious."

"Holy shit."

The boy grinned. "Why don't you come get something to eat? Take a load off. We got pizza. Game's on. Band-Aids are on me, okay?"

Arman nodded. He followed the boy into the far room, opening the Band-Aid box as he went and jamming a few in his pocket before stuffing the rest into his bag. He took a seat at the first table he came to.

The boy hovered. "You doing one of those Walk Across America things? Raising money for dick cancer or something?"

"What?" Arman's head still spun from the twelve-mile revelation. And had the kid said *dick cancer*? "No. I was just, I was at this retreat up the road. But now I want to leave. Walking's the only way to do that."

The boy's smile vanished. "You were at a retreat up the road? You mean that Evolve place?"

"Yeah. That's it. You know about it?"

"I thought only old people went there. My dad says it's for rich retired hippies who want to walk around naked and pretend they've found Paradise."

Arman shrugged. "I don't know. It's not that bad. But there *were* a lot of old people."

"Naked ones?"

"Sort of."

The boy made a face. "I better get back to work."

"Okay."

"You know, maybe you should ask that guy over there for a ride.

He's heading west. Probably leaving soon. Chip in for gas, shouldn't be a problem. He doesn't look too creepy."

Well, that was an underwhelming assessment, but the prospect of a ride wasn't something Arman was about to pass up. He'd sit shotgun to Jeffrey Dahmer if it meant not having to walk around on his blistered feet anymore. "Which guy?"

"Him." The boy pointed.

Arman twisted in his chair. The back door to the barn was open, letting out all the cold air, and sure enough, a guy was out there smoking, on a brick patio where there were more tables and chairs. He sat in the shade, and Arman stared at him. He stared for a good long time, with wide eyes and an open mouth, because this guy, who was wearing dark jeans, cowboy boots, and a polo shirt, who was smoking a cigarette, and who was apparently heading west, was *Beau*.

14

A JUMBLE OF CONFLICTED THOUGHTS ran through Arman's mind. Things like:

What is he doing here?

Is he pissed that I left?

Does he even know that I left?

I'm not sorry for what I did.

I'm not.

But I am sorry I disappointed him.

Arman also recalled what the cook told him that morning, in the warmth of her bed, a moment as far and fleeting as a favorite dream. She'd said that despite everything that had happened, Beau still believed in him. That he still thought Arman was special.

But what do I believe?

And wasn't that the crux of all his problems right there? Because even in the midst of running away, Arman wasn't completely sure if he was leaving because he'd taken a stand or because of his own self-defeating symptoms. His inability to stay in a place where he might actually want to be.

So which was truth?

And which was delusion?

Arman felt tingly. And lost. There was so much in this world he didn't understand. Like who he was. Or where he was going. But what he *did* understand was that an opportunity had presented itself. One he would never have again. So rather than *thinking,* Arman focused on feeling and doing. Like Beau told him to.

What Arman *felt,* he realized, was confusion.

What he could *do,* however, was get up, go outside, and talk to Beau. So he did.

Beau sat beneath a tattered green umbrella that looked as if its heyday had come sometime during the Clinton administration. Although his eyes were open, a long stream of ash curled from the end of his cigarette. It gave the impression that he was sleeping. Or possibly dead. Arman walked over and stood in front of him, but Beau said nothing. He didn't even acknowledge his presence.

Arman's gut knotted. That familiar clench of rejection.

Stop it. No matter what he thinks or what he says, you've already had more than zero effect. You're already something more than nothing.

"Hey," he said cautiously. And when there was no answer: "Hey. It's me, Arman."

This got a response. Beau blinked, then met his gaze. That smooth trademark smile spread across his face, but it came almost a beat too late. Like his reflexes were on tape delay.

Or something.

"*Arman,*" he said. "It's good to see you. Come sit down, won't you?"

Arman hesitated. The sun scorched the back of his neck, the sweltering June air smelled faintly of manure, and something about this situation felt *weird* to him. Unnatural. He couldn't pinpoint it exactly.

But he sat across from Beau. Kept his butt on the very edge of his chair.

"What are you doing here?" he asked.

"Mmmm," Beau said. "Just out for a drive."

Arman frowned. That didn't make sense. Not at all.

"I'm leaving, you know," he said.

"I'm sorry to hear that. Have some water, why don't you? You look hot." Beau pushed an already open bottle toward him.

Arman reached for it gratefully. Took a few gulps, then wiped his mouth. "Well, I'm sorry about last night. I wanted to tell you that. I'm sorry for everything, but especially for throwing that knife of yours. I know it was special."

"More than special," Beau said. "Do you know what it takes to make a knife like that? A true Damascus?"

"I have no idea."

Beau picked up the plastic cap to the water bottle Arman still held and spun it across the table. "The thing you don't see when you look at that kind of blade is that it's not made from a single piece of steel. Or even a single type."

"It's not?"

"No." Beau edged forward in his seat. "You see, the knife maker—and I don't mean just any knife maker, we're talking about a true artist, here—he or she will curate a selection of different metals, stacking them one on top of the next, before heating them all together. Then, when the metal's hot enough, the melted layers are hammered and stretched and folded back in on themselves, before being cut and stacked again. This process repeats over and over. Until the many become one."

"But why?" Arman asked. "Why use all those different metals?"

"Why do you think?"

"I don't know. Does it make the knife stronger or something?"

Beau shrugged. "That's what most people believe."

"But you don't? You don't think that's true?"

"I think it doesn't matter if it's true. The truth is nothing more than proving a lie. That's what the scientific method tells us. But if the blade cuts, you can be sure someone will have faith in its strength."

"Oh," Arman said.

"What else are you sorry for?" Beau asked.

"Huh?"

"Just now. You said you were sorry for everything. But throwing that knife's only one thing."

"Yeah, well, I guess I'm also sorry I let you down. But what you wanted me to do on that mountain, cutting you like that, it seemed *wrong*."

Beau arched an eyebrow. "What gave you the impression you let me down last night?"

"I didn't?"

"That's not what I said."

"Then I don't understand."

"Tell me," Beau said. "Not doing something wrong, that's important to you?"

"Yeah. Sure. Of course it is. I mean, when we're talking about actually *hurting* people or whatever. Then I always want to do the right thing. Morally speaking."

At this, Beau nodded but slumped back in his chair. His river-rock eyes looked sad. Troubled.

"Are you okay?" Arman asked.

Beau waved a hand. "I've got a lot on my mind these days. What I've been trying to do, what I want people to know, it isn't easy. The work is constant. I'm not young anymore. I don't have the luxury of thinking about right or wrong."

"What do you think about?"

"I think about beginnings. And the inevitable end."

"Oh."

Beau dropped his cigarette. Ground it out with his shoe. "Tell me where you're going, Arman. I want to know what the future has in store for you. Bright things, I'm sure. Wondrous things."

Arman squared his shoulders. "I don't know about bright or wondrous. But I'm not going home. I'm not going back to my mom and stepdad. Or any of my family. The rest is a mystery, I guess. I'm walking to the highway. Gonna try and catch a ride. Maybe head down south. We'll see."

Something clicked in Beau's eyes then. They grew stronger. Clearer. "The highway? Why I'll give you a ride. That's too far for you to walk."

"You'd do that?" Relief washed over Arman. "Really?"

"Of course. I told you that you reminded me of myself when I was your age. It's important to me that your journey is paved with kindness."

"Thank you. That's awesome."

"It's nothing. Give me your bag. I'll throw it in the back. And here"—Beau pulled a twenty from his wallet—"why don't you grab something to eat before we go."

"Oh, I can't take your money."

Beau set the bill on the table. Reached for Arman's messenger bag. "I insist. Get some food. When you're ready, we'll hit the road. Van's right there."

Arman glanced over at the parking lot. Sure enough, one of the white passenger vans sat in the shade, collecting dust.

"Okay," he said slowly, picking up the twenty because not picking it up felt rude. He planned to return it, though. Just as soon as he could. "Well, thank you. I'll be right back."

———

Arman headed first to the bathroom to put the Band-Aids he'd stuffed in his pocket on his feet. Some things were more important than food. Once inside, he locked the door and sat on the toilet lid. Then he yanked his shoes and socks off.

And winced.

Ugh. The blisters were worse than he thought. Way worse. They dotted his toes and the bottoms of his feet. The ugliest one sat on the bone jutting out from under his big toe. It bulged from his foot like a frog's eye. Arman gritted his teeth and spent a good five minutes working up the nerve to pop it. When he finally did, all he could think was how unsanitary everything was. No doubt, he was going to get sepsis and die.

After bandaging his feet and getting his shoes back on, Arman scrubbed his hands and face at the sink before he left. He even stuck his head under the faucet and let the cold water run for a while, relishing the chill that ran down his spine and into the small of his back when he finally stood up again. Exhaustion had set in, burrowing into his bones, and he stared at his dripping reflection in the scratched-up mirror. His face was distorted, all stretched and milky. It made his dull features appear more tragic than usual. He yawned at himself.

Then he yawned again.

There was a knock on the door. This was followed by pounding.

Arman turned to fumble with the lock. He had trouble moving his muscles, but he finally got the door open only to find the boy with the blue apron waiting for him in the hallway. The boy's arms were folded, and he didn't look happy. To say the least.

"Oh, hey." Arman stifled another yawn with his hand.

The boy scowled. "I thought you were leaving."

"I am."

"You'd better."

"I just said I was."

"Then move your ass already."

"What's your problem?" Arman asked. "What'd I do?"

"Don't play dumb with me," the boy snapped. "I know what you were doing in there. It's disgusting. That guy told me all about you."

Arman's brain felt thick, the gears churning slowly. "Wait. What are you *talking* about? What did he tell you?"

"You're real lucky, you know that? If my dad were working, you wouldn't be getting off like this. He'd—"

"He'd what?"

The boy's eyes flashed dangerously. "Forget it. Just get the hell out already. And don't let me see your junkie face around here again. Otherwise I'll call him down here. I swear to God I will."

Arman got the hell out. He had no idea what was going on or why, but he knew better than to ask more questions. He knew better than to do anything but turn and go.

Once outside, he hobbled toward the white van. Bolts of pain shot up his calves with each step, and Arman balled his hands into fists. He hated confrontation, but he hated the way that kid had looked at him even more. Like he was worse than nothing. Heat flared within him, a generative rage, and when he reached the passenger side door, Arman yanked it open with a growl. Glared at the driver's seat.

Only no one was there.

Arman stepped back. That was strange. Maybe Beau was smoking again, although, since when did Beau smoke? Arman spun around, holding his hand above his brow. He looked in every direction. Saw nothing but grass. Trees.

The baking sun.

Something felt wrong again. Very wrong. Arman yawned once more as his hands grew clammy. Suddenly the only thing he could think about was what was in the messenger bag he no longer had. All that money.

Why, oh why, had he let Beau take it?

Fuck.

Arman shoved his head back in the van, noticing for the first time that the key was in the ignition. Cool air was blowing and the radio was on. It was playing something country, real moany and sad sounding. He paused and listened for a moment, trying to pick out the words, to see if he knew them.

Something tickled the back of his knuckles just then, the lightest touch. Arman jumped, blinked, then looked down. *What the hell?* It took a moment to register what he was seeing. He was leaning against the passenger seat, but his hands were no longer locked into fists. They were open, relaxed, and he watched, confused, as a brown spider scurried out from under his thumb, bolting straight for the seat cushions. There was also a different song playing on the radio, he realized. No longer moany, it was now something upbeat and catchy.

Arman felt ill. Seriously ill. Something really was wrong with him. With his brain. That's what it felt like. It was almost as if he'd fallen asleep—he even had drool on his chin—but he was still standing, so that couldn't be it. He shook his head. Well, whatever had happened or how, a piece of time had apparently just skipped away from him—a loss he had no way of finding because he couldn't remember anything other than tipping his face into the cool air, wondering where the hell Beau was. Arman rubbed his eyes. Maybe he needed to lie down in the back of the van for a minute. Maybe he needed to—

Arman froze.

In the back of the van.

He jerked his head out of the cab. Stood upright. The sun blinded him, stoking his resentment and dumping more sweat down his neck. Arman wobbled a bit, his legs unsteady, but managed to walk back to the van's side door. With a grunt and a heave, he used both hands to pry it open.

What he saw inside made him go cold.

Oh God. No. Oh no. This can't be happening.

It can't.

But it was. Horribly. And what was it Beau had said to him earlier?

I think about beginnings.

And the inevitable end.

NOTHING MORE.

Every system has a purpose. But purpose is not the same as having a plan.

When the heart pumps blood or the atom splits or the last train out of the city departs five minutes late, there's a reason these actions occur. But reason has nothing to do with wants. Or needs. Or strategy.

Or even fate.

Like the unraveling of the most twisted lie, meaning works backward. The end can explain the means, but nothing is ever justified. Systems are not in the business of morality. They exist to serve themselves. This is the reason inequity breeds cruelty, shame fosters compliance, and hypocrisy creates denial.

These are systems that work.

There are other systems, too. Everywhere, all around us. Ones we operate within, ones we choose to chafe against, and ones we don't even know how to see. They exist nonetheless. They assert their will upon every aspect of our lives—from the smallest parts of our world to the fever-dream depths of our humanity to the ragged edges of the universe. And beyond.

Death is a system, too, of course. But that's an easy one.

Don't you see?

With death comes the end of life.

That's all.

There's nothing more.

15

OH, BEAU.

Why'd you do it? Why?

This isn't kindness.

This isn't the road either of us should be on.

Blood poured down Arman's forehead. It dripped into his line of vision, mixing with his tears and his snot, but he didn't bother wiping any of it away. He just kept driving as best he could, racing the white van back up the mountain toward the compound. He had the gas pedal pressed to the floor. He had his arms locked tight. Arman wasn't used to handling a vehicle of this size—hell, he wasn't used to *driving*, period—and that meant he took the curves too wide and the hills too fast. Tires screeched and the vehicle swayed, but he didn't slow down. He kept going. And going.

He *had* to.

The iron gate was open when he got there. With a sob of relief, Arman cut the wheel to make the turn. The van lurched, then skidded before regaining traction. It chewed up the drive like a beast.

Arman didn't bother parking in the designated lot or anywhere he was meant to. He flew past all the other vans and headed up the hillside straight for the domed building, leaning on the horn the whole way. But the road soon grew steep and narrow, and when the wheels spun helplessly in the gravel, he had no choice but to slam on the brake, throw the van into park, and jump out.

Staggering on legs weak and shaky, he cupped his hands. Managed to shout, "Hey! I need help! Please! *Someone!*"

There was no response. The only sound was the faint rustling of the long grass as a gust of ocean wind fluttered up the mountainside, cool as a promise in the late-day heat.

Arman took off running. Adrenaline coursed through him as he bounded up the path and sprinted for the dome on winged feet. His legs burned with each stride and his lungs strained like bellows as he breathed in the heady scent of licorice and eucalyptus. The wood smoke puffing from the towering chimney.

It all filled him with the oddest sense of déjà vu.

He kept running. The doors to the meeting hall were shut. Arman grabbed the handle of the first one he came to and pulled. It opened, thankfully, and he flew inside with a tingle of relief. His world went from light to dark.

"Hey!" he called out, gasping for air. "Is anyone here? I need help. I need someone. It's an *emergency!*"

The unexpected happened: A pair of strong arms reached from the shadows to grab on to Arman. They caught him like a trip wire, wrapping around his chest, his shoulders, and stopping him in his tracks.

Arman gave a yelp of pain. He was yanked backward and his feet skidded, nearly upending him. He thrashed wildly against whoever was holding him. "*Fuck.* Fucking let *go* of me!"

"Shut up," snarled the person who'd grabbed him, gripping him tighter and pinning his arms to his body like a straitjacket.

Arman kept up his thrashing. "*What?*"

"I said shut up. You can't come in here. Where the hell did you come from anyway?"

"What do you *mean?*" Squirming sideways, Arman caught a glimpse of his accoster. The sunlight spilling down from the cribbed rafters in the center of the dome didn't reach here, the edges of the hall, but as his eyes adjusted to the darkness, he was able to make out the shape of the man holding on to him. He was big, brutish, and he wore those strange gauzy clothes. Arman thought he could feel something beneath the fabric, like a holster, running across his chest. Panic filled him. Maybe Dale wasn't kidding about guns.

"This is private property, kid," the man growled.

"But—"

"Is something going on, Brian?" a woman's voice called out.

They both turned. Arman's heart surged with hope. It was *Mari.* She was standing on some sort of stage that had been set up in the center of the domed space, built against the crackling stone fireplace. Not only that, but she was surrounded by rows and rows of people who were seated in folding chairs, filling the entire room.

She was surrounded, Arman realized with a stab of terror, by *everyone.*

"Mari!" he cried. "It's me, Arman. I need your help!"

"What is it, Arman?" she asked. Then: "Brian, let go of him, for God's sake. He's one of ours."

Brian released Arman but made sure to knee him in the back as he shoved him away. Arman stumbled, then squared his shoulders. Longed for the nerve to punch him. Instead he limped forward into the sunlight.

He felt all the eyes in the room land on him.

He heard the gasps when they saw the blood on his face and clothes.

Stomach lodged in his throat like a cork, Arman willed himself not to fall apart. Not yet. Not before he'd done what he'd come to do. He locked eyes with Mari because seeing her calmed him. Because even though he'd burst in and caused this big scene, she still looked at him with kindness.

And trust.

"It's Beau," he said, his voice finally cracking. "I think—I think he's *dead*."

A swell of shock rippled through the meeting hall. Followed by fear. Then disbelief. Arman didn't know what to do, so he simply stood and waited. He felt twitchy. And more than a little queasy. He hadn't realized how *hot* it was in here. All these bodies packed in tight with limited air circulation. The smell wasn't very good either.

Finally Mari raised her hand, quieting the room with the gesture. Arman watched with awe. Despite her age and gentle demeanor, she was far more commanding than he would've guessed. Or perhaps those qualities weren't the exception, but the rule.

"I'm sure Beau is fine," she told her audience. "As you know, he was called away from us this morning on an emergency in San Francisco and won't be returning until tomorrow. However, seeing as young Arman here is one of our newer guests, the three of us are going to go with him now to help clarify what's happened and see how we can best help him. While we're gone, I'd like you all to remain seated and in a state of quiet self-reflection. Inoculation will resume momentarily."

Three of us? Arman's heart sank as two people stood and followed Mari as she stepped off the stage and walked toward him. He recognized them both, of course. He should've known: It was the short man and the dark-haired woman who'd scolded Mari for asking where he'd come from.

Beau's not *fine,* Arman wanted to tell them as they headed outside and back onto the dirt path, with him leading the way like the world's most unlikely Pied Piper. But the words wouldn't come. He was too tight with emotion.

Too sick with guilt.

Making him feel even sicker was the way his heart gummed up upon reaching the crest of the road that dipped down toward where he'd left the van. His grief was kicking in at last, he thought. Finally overriding the numbness and shock.

"Come on," he called, waving to those behind him. "He's right here."

Mari and the other two hurried to catch up, as best they could, although for Mari, moving quickly clearly wasn't something in her aging body's current skill set. Arman turned to start down the steep-pitched hillside. Only he took one step and he stopped. And blinked.

Because it wasn't there.

The van wasn't there.

It was gone.

16

ARMAN STUMBLED DOWN THE PATH in a state of utter confusion. He *knew* he'd parked the van here. He knew it. Yet there was no sign of it at all. No sign that it had even *been* here in the first place. He scoured the ground for clues. After a moment of squinting, he thought he could make out faint tire tracks in the dirt.

But maybe not.

It was too hard to tell.

He straightened up again. The van's brakes could have gone out, he realized. That would explain things. The hill behind him was angled sharply. It would've gone right over the side of the road.

Arman rushed to look. The trajectory of the runaway van would've sent it down the embankment and straight into a patch of manzanita and scrub brush. Only it wasn't there. And it wasn't in the parking lot, either. Well, there were plenty of white vans in the lot, of course, a whole row of them, but when Arman ran past and placed a hand on each of their hoods, all their engines were cool. None was the vehicle he'd just driven up here in a wild panic, no more than fifteen minutes ago. *That* van was gone.

Poof.

Arman stood, frozen. He didn't know what to do. He didn't know where else to look.

Am I losing my mind?

Am I?

That's what it felt like.

Mari, the short man, and the dark-haired woman followed him wherever he went and watched him closely. Expressions of concern were etched across their faces.

Doubt, too.

"I thought you said Beau was down here," the dark-haired woman said finally.

"He *was*."

"And he was dead."

"Yes. I think so. I mean, I'm pretty sure." Arman put a fluttering hand to his head. His memories of the recent past felt foggy. Distant.

He wasn't, he realized, all that sure of anything.

"So where is he now?" the woman asked.

"I don't know. Someone—someone must've found him. The keys were still in the van. Maybe they took him somewhere. To a hospital."

She gave him a withering look. "And who would've done that? Everyone was in the meeting hall just now. Every single person. Except you."

"Are you saying you don't believe me?"

"I'm saying there's nothing to believe."

This was stupid. Arman pulled at his shirt. Pointed to it emphatically. "And where do you think all this blood came from?"

The woman shrugged. "Your bleeding head? Just a guess."

"He was *here*! The van was here!" Arman shouted. He couldn't help himself.

"Well, he's not here now."

"Then someone must have come in from the outside and found him!"

"Impossible," the short man said. "No one drives up here. Road's a dead end. No one even knows we're here."

Sure they do, Arman started to say, thinking of the boy at the market. But he couldn't get the words out. His whole body started to shake. Great seismic shudders that emanated from deep within him.

Oh, Beau. Beau. I'm sorry. I'm so sorry.

Mari came over and rubbed the back of his neck. Arman let her. Her concern soothed him in a way he didn't know how to describe, spooling some desperate need from his heart to her hands. *I don't understand what's happening,* he longed to tell her. *Please help me understand.*

"He was here," Arman said again, but his voice had lost its gusto. Could he really have been mistaken about Beau being dead in the first place? Maybe he'd driven himself somewhere. Maybe he was fine. Maybe Arman had gotten this whole thing all wrong.

But there was all that blood. So much of it. And the knife. Oh God, the knife—

His shaking grew worse, until his teeth chattered and his mouth grew watery. Until he had to sit on the ground and put his head between his legs. Mari crouched beside him, hand still on his neck, and while Arman focused on breathing deeply and not passing out, drifts of conversation between her and the dark-haired woman floated above him.

"—confused, in shock, maybe drugs of some sort—"

"—need to get back. This is taking too much damn time—"

"—head wound. Possible brain injury, memory loss—"

"Hey, is this yours?" a male voice called out.

Arman lifted his head. Maybe twenty yards away, the short man stood beneath a thick-barked eucalyptus tree, and he had something in his hands. Arman stared. For a moment he was unable to make out what it was, but then realization hit him.

"Yes! That's my bag! That's *mine*." He pointed, looking up at the other two. "See. I *told* you. That was in the van. Someone took the van and they left my bag. I'm not making this up!"

The short man walked over and handed the bag to Arman. He dug through it frantically, clothes spilling on the ground. A moan of relief escaped him. The money was still there. All of it.

The dark-haired woman watched him. "Were you planning on going somewhere?"

"I *did* go somewhere. I already told you that!"

"Why don't you just tell us everything that happened, Arman," Mari said with a sigh. "Start at the beginning."

So that's what he did. He took a deep breath and told them how he'd left the compound before dawn that morning and started his walk back toward civilization. He told them how he'd run into Beau at the market and that Beau was going to give him a ride to the highway. And—leaving out the part where Beau told the kid at the store Arman was a junkie and that strange moment of lost time—he told them how before they could drive anywhere together, the most horrible thing had happened: Arman had found Beau's lifeless body in the back of the van. And it wasn't due to any kind of accident or foul play. No, while Arman had been in the bathroom dicking around with his blisters and his Band-Aids, lamenting over the dullness of his looks, apparently Beau had been in the van cutting open his wrists and bleeding out all over the damn place.

The wrists I wouldn't cut.

With the knife I wouldn't use.

Everything after was a nightmare, moments too hazy and fractured for Arman to recall in detail. All he had were bright bursts of memory: the blood-soaked van; Beau's gray face and slack neck.

But that was it.

"Why on earth would Beau kill himself?" the dark-haired woman asked. "What possible reason would he have to do that?"

"I don't know *why*. But he, uh, seemed kind of weird when I talked to him."

"'*Kind of weird?*' Is that a technical term?"

Arman glared.

"What did he cut himself with?" the short man asked. "I don't remember you saying."

"That's because I didn't say."

"Then what was it?"

"It was this knife. Beau had it last night. He said it was his grandfather's. A Damascus, he called it. It's got this thick blade, and there's a pattern to the metal. Like a fingerprint."

At this, a look passed between the three adults. Arman didn't know what it meant. But he saw it. Clear as day.

"What?" he asked. "What is it?"

"But that knife—" started the short man.

"You threw it over a cliff last night, didn't you?" finished the dark-haired woman. "We heard about that. Beau told us. It was an heirloom. Irreplaceable."

"It was. I did."

"Then how could he have had it?"

"I don't know." Arman faltered. After all, it didn't make sense to him either.

"Arman, how did you hurt your head?" Mari asked.

His fingers went to the wound on his temple. "I—I don't remember."

"You don't remember?"

"I think I was running. Maybe I blacked out or something." He looked at her. "All I know is that I thought—I thought I could still *help* him. I wanted to try. I had to try."

"So did you call the police? Or try to find a hospital?"

"I couldn't! My phone didn't work! And the kid working at the market in Los Padres wouldn't let me use his. He didn't like me."

"Did you go anywhere else?" Mari asked. "Or talk to anyone?"

"No."

"But how can you be sure if you don't even remember hurting yourself?"

"I just am," Arman said. "I came here. I came right here. I know that."

Mari didn't respond. But she looked worried.

"You know," the dark-haired woman began, and she spoke in the sort of taunting tone that made Arman want to poke her eyes out. "This whole thing reminds me of a movie I once saw where this woman goes to pick her child up from nursery school, only it turns out nobody's ever seen her child. Nobody even knew she *had* one and the kid's not enrolled at the school. She never was. Then the mother goes home and finds that all of her child's things are missing. There's no trace of the kid anywhere. Gary, do you know the one I'm talking about?"

The short man—Gary—nodded. "*Bunny Lake Is Missing.*"

The dark-haired woman smiled. "That's right. Bunny Lake. You're like Bunny Lake's mother."

"What happened to her?" Arman asked cautiously.

"People thought she was crazy, of course. She was looking for something that didn't exist."

"What are you talking about? Beau exists. You know he exists."

The dark-haired woman waved a hand. "You're telling us to believe in the existence of something you have no proof of. It's the same thing, really."

Arman squeezed his hands into fists to keep from digging into his own skin. "It's not the same thing! The *proof* is that the van is missing!"

"'Absence of evidence is not evidence of absence,'" Gary recited in a singsong voice.

Now Arman wanted to poke his own eyes out. He knew that old maxim. He knew it well. Last year, his physics teacher had had a poster with those same words hanging in the back of his classroom.

"Well, shouldn't we call the cops now?" he asked. "Let them figure things out?"

The dark-haired woman was still smiling. "And tell them what exactly?"

"I don't know," Arman said, and even he felt his resolve dissipating. Considering the money in his bag and the blood all over him and the fact that a lot of people had seen him argue with Beau last night, talking to the cops was not high on his list of desirable activities. Even if it was the right thing to do.

Which it probably was.

But Mari, it seemed, could read his mind. And as always, she was gracious. "Arman, no matter what happened, you did the right thing. Okay? Going to the police or anyone else would've been confusing. They wouldn't have understood you. So please don't feel bad."

Arman nodded.

"I think you should lie down and rest now," she said gently. "You hit your head pretty hard. That could explain why you're confused."

"Lie down where?" Arman asked.

"You don't remember where you're staying?"

"No, I *do*. It's just . . ."

"It's just what?"

Arman looked at her with pleading eyes. "It's just nothing about this . . . well, nothing makes *sense.*"

"Of course it makes sense," Mari told him in the kindest way possible. Then she echoed the exact words the cook had spoken to Arman earlier that morning, "You just don't know how."

17

ARMAN WAS IN A DAZE. A wretched one. What else could he do but accept that he was either completely delusional and had imagined the last six hours of his life or . . .

Or *what?*

Or nothing, he realized. There wasn't any other option. He was batshit crazy. He had to be. Because dead bodies didn't disappear and vans didn't vanish into thin air and heirloom knives didn't return from the depths of darkness.

Except when they did.

Hence the daze.

The adults standing around Arman kept talking. And they did it in that way adults always did. Like they knew best. Somehow it was decided that Gary would walk with Arman back up to the cabin where he'd been staying. Gary was a doctor, it turned out, a real medical doctor, and he wanted to tend to Arman's head wound. Apparently there was a first aid station somewhere up there, too.

Doctor or no doctor, Arman did *not* want to walk with him—he didn't like the guy's arrogance or his drippy voice or even the way his weird gauzy clothes dragged on the ground because his legs were too short for his body—but Arman was in no position to argue. Both Mari and the dark-haired woman insisted. Only there was something about their insistence that felt off to Arman. Like he was being pandered to. Or appeased. He resented that. There was a stark difference, he thought, in being cared for and being taken care of.

But in the end, Arman agreed—because it wasn't a choice and really never had been—and started the walk back up to the cabin with Dr. Gary at his side, carrying his bag for him.

"You're going to need stitches," the doctor told him.

"Really?" Arman had never had stitches. The idea wasn't a pleasant one, thinking of his body as unwillingly open. Exposed to the world for everyone to see.

"We'll need to go to the research building for that. I don't keep all that equipment in my cabin."

"What research building?"

"You'll see."

They walked more. Arman got the feeling the dislike between them was a mutual thing, but the silence made him grow restless.

"What's going on in there?" He pointed back toward the domed meeting hall, which was still visible over the tall grass and the wildflowers blanketing the meadow.

Dr. Gary gave a terse nod. "That's Inoculation. It's a long process."

"How long?"

"They'll be there until at least dinner."

"But what are they doing exactly?"

"Well, to be fully Inoculated, you first have to identify what it is that's making you sick. We don't target symptoms here; we work on a model of vector control. So that's what they're doing. Identifying where disease transmission is occurring in their Outside Lives, so that they can put a stop to it."

"Hmm." Arman thought of the disarray his own mind and body were in. What vectors were responsible for *his* disease? His parents, he supposed, but it had to be more than that. When Arman closed his eyes and pictured himself as a dot in the center of a bull's-eye, surrounded by all the systems he operated within on a daily basis—home, school, his social life, youth group, basketball, the entire US government—the number of possible vectors affecting him seemed infinite. But didn't that mean Occam's razor should apply? If *everything* made him miserable, wasn't the likely origin of the problem him?

No. Stop it. There's nothing wrong with you. That type of thinking is why you came here in the first place. It's why you need to change.

It's why you need Beau.

Except Beau was gone and possibly dead, and Arman, in his effort to run away, was the one who'd lost him. And wasn't that the strongest evidence that there was something wrong with him?

Didn't that prove, deep down, in the most empirical of ways, that he was a bad person?

"What are you thinking about, Arman?" Dr. Gary's cool voice sliced its way into his daydream.

Arman twitched. "Nothing."

"You seem upset."

"I *am* upset."

"We teach that, too, you know. How to regulate your emotions. How to remain rational in times of crisis so that you can choose the correct path toward healing."

"Aren't *you* supposed to heal people?" Arman asked with a glare. "I mean, seeing as you're a doctor and all."

Dr. Gary's lips widened into the most placid of smiles. "You're right. I am a doctor. But where much of the medical work I do is reparative, the work we do here is *empowering*. You see, not only are we trying to help individuals evolve to a place where they can manage their own immune systems, but we also know it's possible for people in very heightened states of consciousness to control *all* planes of existence: physical, emotional, spiritual. That's true independence. That's *freedom*. There'll be no need for doctors at that point."

Arman was doubtful. "There won't?"

"Oh no. I mean, we're not there yet. But that's where we're going. That's going to be the next phase."

"Next phase in what?"

"The *evolution*. The one happening right here." The doctor gestured out at the compound property. "Our first phase has been focused on recruiting and training. On building our base. But now we need to go further."

"How?"

"The way all research is done. Or at least the way it should be. With *control*. By closing our borders and becoming completely self-sufficient, we'll be able to maintain a sterile environment. There'll be no contamination from the outside world. Our Enforcement strategy will make sure of that. And that's when our work will really begin."

"Beau didn't say anything about closing the compound."

"Beau's been focusing on growth. That's really his area of strength. But he'll come around. It's going to be beautiful, Arman. When the mind and body achieve true harmony, there will be no limits. None. You can be or do anything."

Arman didn't know what to say. The whole thing sounded strange. And not all that appealing, if he was being honest. He'd come here to learn how to deal with the outside world, not live with a bunch of old people forever. What would happen when they all died? "You know, I'm only supposed to be here a week."

"Oh, I'm sure you will be," the doctor said soothingly. "We're being very selective about who stays for this phase. It's not for everyone. It's going to take a lot of resources."

They kept hiking and Dr. Gary kept talking, though Arman had long stopped listening. As they passed the cluster of cabins where Arman had been staying, Dr. Gary led them into the woods, veering off the main trail to brush beneath the low-hung branches of pine trees. Arman followed reluctantly, staring up the hillside. The cook's house wasn't much farther, just a few hundred feet, and despite his confusion, he refused to believe those breathless, urgent moments between them that morning had been anything but real. There'd been no dream, no fantasy, he'd ever had that had felt like *that*.

Finally they reached the two-story, flat-roofed building Arman had noticed yesterday on his way to the bathroom. The one with the dark windows.

"What is this place?" he asked. Unlike the rest of the compound, there was nothing warm or rustic about the building. It was institutional. Bland. It exuded gloom. "People don't sleep here, do they?"

The doctor pulled a set of keys from his pocket to unlock the front door. "Here? No. It's used for storage mostly, these days. But I do keep an office here."

"An office?"

"That's sort of a joke. It's not like I have a lot of patients."

"But you called it a research building."

"Well, that's what it used to be. Back in the day. When Beau was actually interested in that sort of thing."

"What kind of research?"

"Human potential."

Once inside, they headed down a long corridor that reminded Arman of the administrative wing of his grungy high school. It reeked of depression and foregone dreams. Passing by shut door after shut door, he noticed names had been painted above each entryway: JUSTICE. MERCY. PRIDE. RESISTANCE. All virtues, it seemed, although not necessarily Christian ones. He tried peeking into one of the small windows only to find it painted black.

"What's in there?" he asked.

"I told you. Storage."

"But why are the windows painted?"

"You ask a lot of questions, don't you?"

Arman cringed. "Sorry."

The doctor's office was at the end of the hall. The word above his door was WISDOM, which Arman found reassuring. Again Dr. Gary used his key ring, switching on the overhead light, ushering Arman in.

Surprised, Arman looked around. The space was far bigger than he'd imagined, and while the surfaces were dusty and the air stale, it was definitely nicer than the doctor's office he went to back at home—the one with the waiting room full of shrieking children, surly teens, and stressed-out mothers. This room was large, open, and flooded with dappled light coming in through the plate-glass windows that looked out over the hills and toward the ocean beyond.

"Have a seat." Dr. Gary gestured to the black leather chair set in the center of the room.

Arman took a step toward the chair. Then hesitated.

"I know this all seems a little out of place," Dr. Gary said. "But like I told Beau, if I'm going to work here, really work, it needs to be my *best* work. That's why I've brought all of this equipment down here and why I wanted to set up my office in a space with real amenities. In the long run, it helps to keep us independent."

Arman sat tentatively in the chair while Dr. Gary cleared his desk, shoving books and papers, even a laptop, onto the floor and into boxes. Then he turned toward the far wall. Began opening cabinets, setting items on a metal tray.

"What kind of doctor did you say you were?" Arman asked.

"Those questions again."

"Forget it."

"No, it's okay. I was trained in emergency medicine. Did ER work for years. Trauma. I knew it was what I wanted to do since I was a kid. I've always been good in a crisis. Level-headed. And I loved it at first. The power of saving people. Of having answers. But over time I realized I wasn't saving anything. Sure I could bring a heart-attack victim back to life or take a bullet out of an organ, but by the time those people got to me, the damage had already been done. I was the solution for failure, which really isn't an answer at all."

"Oh." Arman picked at a hangnail he thought might be growing infected. He was sorry he'd asked anything in the first place. It wasn't like he'd wanted to hear the guy's life story.

"Are you allergic to any medications?" the doctor asked.

"No."

"Are you currently taking any?"

"Isn't that against the rules? Taking medication?"

Dr. Gary tipped his head. "Good to know you've been paying attention to something around here."

Arman didn't respond.

"Now, how bad would you say your headache is right now, on a scale of one to ten?" the doctor asked.

"A seven, I guess."

"Do you know what day it is?"

"Sunday."

"What state are we in?"

"California."

"Good. How's your vision? Seeing double? Anything out of focus or just feel not right?"

"Not really."

"Any nausea? Vomiting?"

Arman shook his head.

"Did you lose consciousness when you got hurt?"

"I don't remember."

"What about confusion? Any disorientation? Having trouble understanding what's going on around you?"

"Well, yes. Yes and yes. You know that."

"These symptoms are fairly common with concussions. So is memory loss."

"So what does that mean?"

"I'm not sure it *means* anything. I'm just trying to explain why you're confused."

"But you actually think it's possible that I somehow hit my head and imagined this whole thing? Everything that happened today?"

"Definitely possible. Although it might indicate that there's other stress going on in your life at the moment, as well."

"Like what?"

"I don't know. I'm not that kind of doctor."

Arman bit back a laugh. Stared up at the ceiling. "So I'm crazy. That's what you're saying?"

Dr. Gary sat on a rolling stool. Pushed himself close to Arman until their knees were touching. "Look, I understand you had experiences today that felt real to you. But I also know that memory can be a tricky thing. It doesn't always tell the truth the way we think it does."

"But—"

"Beau's *fine*, Arman. Trust me on that. You'll see tomorrow when he returns. Meanwhile, you're going to rest. Head injuries can take a long time to heal. Now I want you to stare at the wall behind me." He pulled a penlight from the tray and flashed it into Arman's eyes. After a moment, he rolled back. Handed him two pills and a cup of water.

Arman looked at the pills. "What are these?"

"They're to help with the pain you're feeling. Acute injury is one of the few times we make allowances for medication. Are you hurt anywhere else?"

"My feet have blisters," Arman said. Then he sat up. "Hold on. Look in my bag, will you? There should be a box of Band-Aids in there, right on top. They're from that market. That'll at least prove I was there!"

"The Los Padres Market?"

"Yes!"

Dr. Gary went and got Arman's bag from where it sat on the floor. He unclipped the front flap, opened it, and held it in front of Arman.

There were no Band-Aids.

Of course there weren't.

Arman slouched back. He placed the pills he'd been handed into his mouth and swallowed them.

"Are you okay?" Dr. Gary asked.

"I don't know what I am."

"Then it's no wonder you're struggling with the program."

"What's that supposed to mean?"

"Just what I said. Now why don't you tilt your head to the right for me." Dr. Gary pulled on a pair of rubber gloves, then switched on a portable light that nearly blinded Arman. "Go ahead and close your eyes. I'm going to rinse and clean the wound. Then I'll give you a small shot of anesthetic before I stitch it up. The whole thing should be real easy. Okay?"

Arman nodded. He hated needles, but didn't want to say that. He was long past his childhood days of cowering and hiding under tables from nurses, but that didn't mean he wasn't scared. Although, at the moment, he realized, with his sanity in doubt, he was more scared of *himself* than anything else. That was a terrible feeling. The worst.

So Arman did what he was told.

He leaned back in the chair.

He closed his eyes.

18

"JESUS. YOU LOOK LIKE SHIT." At the sight of Arman appearing in the cabin doorway, Dale leapt off his cot like he'd sat in a nest of spiders. A gray haze of pot smoke swirled around his head.

Arman didn't move from where he stood. His brain felt empty. Scraped clean. He didn't think he wanted to know what Dale had been doing before he'd interrupted him. He didn't think he wanted to know anything. He just wanted to sleep. "Huh?"

Dale, who was simultaneously grinding a joint out on the dusty floorboards with one of Kira's high-heeled sandals, waved Arman inside. "Well, sit down or something. Christ. You look like the walking dead. And is that *blood*? Gross, man."

Arman stepped inside the cabin. Then he stopped. Stared down at his T-shirt. Sure enough, there was blood streaked across the front of it.

"Oh yeah," he said. "I hit my head."

Dale came toward him then, removing his sunglasses and inspecting him closely, red-rimmed eyes running from head to toe. "Fuck. Are those *stitches*? What happened? Who did that?"

"A doctor did it. The stitches, I mean."

"*A doctor did it?* That's all you're gonna say?"

"His name's Gary." Arman took a breath. "Sorry if I'm being spacey. He gave me some kind of painkiller. I can't think too straight right now."

"A painkiller, huh? Well, I hope he gave you something good. Like morphine. Or Percocet." Dale paused. "Did he?"

"I don't know."

"Did you get any more?"

"No."

Dale sighed. "Well, tell me what you've been doing all day then. Kira's been worried. She thought you'd been Jonestowned or something."

"And you weren't worried?"

"Nah. I don't worry about a lot of things. It's nothing personal."

"Where is Kira?" Arman looked around. She definitely wasn't anywhere in the cabin.

"She's still down at that stupid meeting. She's really into it, this whole thing, the whole program, all the denouncing your family—excuse me, your *vectors*—and finding wellness within. Figures. She's the one who wanted to come in the first place. Not me. My family's not worth denouncing. I mean, it's not like they would care, so what's the point?"

"But you're not at Inoculation," Arman said, which wasn't a question, but an observation about something that seemed wrong. *Everybody* was supposed to be at Inoculation.

Right?

"Well, you're not there either." Dale lowered his voice. "And just between us, I think it's all a bunch of bullshit. That Beau guy wasn't even there today, but it didn't matter. Those so-called trainers jumped in all eager, leading the speeches, telling us we need to *commit to the program* or else. Like they were glad he was gone. They bring people here, too, you know. I bet we could if we wanted to. Get paid for our effort. They're just a bunch of con artists, man. All of them."

Arman's head snapped up. "What did you say?"

"I'm saying it's a total scam. Everything here. This morning we stayed in that room for *hours* while they yelled at us. They wouldn't let us eat. Wouldn't even let me take a piss."

"Seriously?"

"Seriously. Apparently bodily functions are against the rules. Deodorant, too. I snuck out during one of the group confessional things when no one was looking. They were making people stand up in front of everybody and talk about all the ways people in their lives were toxic. It sucked. People were crying and shit. Some lady *fainted.*"

Arman put a hand to his heart.

"What's wrong?" Dale asked.

"I need to sit down."

"Didn't I tell you that already?" Dale gestured for Arman to sit on the cot, which he did. He let the heavy messenger bag drop from his shoulder to the floor with a thud.

"You all right?" Dale asked after a moment. "You must've hit your head pretty hard."

"Yeah."

"You know, you still haven't told me how you did it. Or what you've been doing all day."

"I don't know what I've been doing all day," Arman said. "That's just it. I thought I knew. But I don't anymore. I don't think I know anything."

"I think I know you're really stoned right now. You sound like a god-damn robot."

"Sorry."

"Don't be."

"Hey, Dale?"

"Hey, what?"

"Have you ever had something happen only to realize later that none of it was real? That it couldn't be real?"

"You talking about acid? Don't get into that shit."

"No, not acid."

"What then?"

Arman sighed. "Forget it. I need to sleep."

"Hey, were you *going* somewhere?" Dale was staring at his bag.

Arman nodded, collapsing onto his side with a yawn. He didn't have the energy to stay upright any longer. "This morning. I tried to leave this morning."

"Why? You already paid to be here. You got room and board, man. The people are weird, but people are always weird. There's a good view. The air's fresh."

"Because I'm a fuck-up," Arman said. "Because Beau wanted me to do something last night and I didn't do it. Because I don't want to *keep* fucking up."

Dale snorted. "Pretty ironic then, huh?"

"What do you mean?"

"I mean, seeing as you tried to leave and you ended up back here anyway, it kinda looks like you fucked that up, too."

HOPE YOU CAN.

They show up right on time and right in the order you told them to. The two guys arrive first, followed by the dark-haired girl. You can't help but admire her confidence as she walks in. She's serious, ready to do battle, even though this is far from a war. You can read her determination because she's got her hair pulled back and doesn't once look at her phone. She's smarter than the boys, and she's going to make sure they know it.

You wonder again why she doesn't smoke and what it could mean. Not that it matters much in the long run.

But it might.

When it comes time for you to start, you don't play favorites. Your audience is rapt and your job is to keep it that way. You talk and you talk, and soon the expressions on their faces become the ones you anticipate. There's awe. Affirmation. Followed by the desire for approval.

Yours, of course.

You talk more and they keep listening. But all the while, you're listening, too. Group dynamics are your specialty. You glean information from every silence and passing glance until you know just what drives each one of them. Until you know how to play them to your advantage.

Young people are the easiest to read, you've found, still pliable, still eager. And these three have been taught well, at least for your purposes. They're products of their time, willing to take on debt and more debt with no job in sight because they don't know any other way to try. Individualism is their birthright, their false ideal. This means they've learned to question the truth, but never their dreams, and that above all else, they believe deeply in what they want to see, not the image that's right in front of them.

What they want, of course, isn't what you can give them.

What you're selling is the hope you can.

19

ARMAN'S DREAMS WERE ALL NIGHTMARES.

In them, he was sliding open the van door. He was seeing the blood. It was everywhere, great quantities of it, spilling from Beau's arms, dripping, pooling like a lake, reminding Arman of a video he'd seen in which a hockey player's throat was sliced by a skate on the ice, severing his carotid artery and flooding the crease with his blood. The player's life had been saved by a quick-acting doctor, but Arman wasn't a doctor.

He wasn't *anything*.

It doesn't matter what you are, damnit. Help him already!

Get a tourniquet.

Stop the bleeding.

Do something!

Only Arman didn't help or get or stop. Instead a gleam of light jolted him from his state of shock. A flash. A glint. The gleaming object lay on the van's floor, right at Beau's feet. Arman's vision swam to see what it was—a knife. A knife he *knew*, its polished layers of steel having been hammered into the most delicate of designs. The whole thing now splashed with red.

That's not possible. It's not. That knife can't be here.

I threw it away.

Then the dream shuttled forward. One minute Arman was staring down at the floor, at a knife that didn't belong, the next he was leaping out of the van in a feral burst of panic and sunlight, sprinting for the market's back door. There was pain in his head, a sickening ache, and blood was in his eyes and streaming down his face, only he didn't know why it was there. He didn't know how he'd been hurt.

The barn door was locked. Arman bolted around to the front of the store, only to find that that door was locked, too. And all the lights were off. Despite his growing pain and growing weakness, he pounded on the glass and shouted for the boy he knew was inside to open up. Only he didn't. Asshole.

I need to get help. An ambulance.

A medic.

Someone!

But the longer Arman stood banging on the door and pleading for compassion that wasn't forthcoming, the more certain he became that at any moment the cops were going to show up. They were going to pull into the parking lot, and they were going to find Beau and the blood and Arman's bleeding head and his bag that was filled with thousands of stolen dollars. The boy with the blue apron would probably have something to say about it all, too. The cops would start asking questions, lots of questions, and Arman didn't think he'd like the conclusions they'd come to.

At all.

So of all the choices Arman could make in that moment, it was by far the easiest and most cowardly to turn and jog back to the white van that sat in the shade with the engine still running; to avoid looking at Beau or the knife, much less touch either of them; to hastily shut the side passenger doors and crawl into the driver's seat; to back the vehicle out of the parking lot onto the main road and to head right back up to the compound.

Arman woke with a gasp.

He sat straight up. Looked around. Recognition took its sweet time, but he soon figured out that he was on his cot, alone in the cabin, with his heart racing. Hummingbird fast. And he was soaked with sweat.

You're awake now. It was just a dream.

But his despair failed to dissipate. Dreaming had done nothing to change reality. It hadn't made him less of a coward or lightened the weight of his guilt.

Oh Beau.

A strange scent wafted across the cabin then. Fragrant and earthy, it caught Arman's attention. Paused his guilt spiral. It was a good smell, too, with just a hint of richness. Like the most comforting of food. The scent floated across the cabin, filling his nostrils, teasing his mind like magic, and conjuring up the distant dance of memories he'd kept long buried: warm meals around the dinner table in the time before his parents' divorce, back when his father was still around and still doing his best to stay honest. Or at least give the *impression* of honesty.

Giving impressions, after all, was sort of his thing.

With bleary eyes, Arman searched for the source of the smell. It came from a wicker picnic basket that had been set on the table in the center of the room. That was strange, he thought. The basket hadn't been there earlier, when he was talking to Dale. He would've noticed it. And he *had* talked to Dale earlier, hadn't he?

It was hard to remember.

Arman got up, wincing as he stood. Not only were his feet sore, but moving brought back the ache in his head, deep enough to hitch his breath. He fingered his stitches gratefully. Despite the pain, the presence of his blisters and the head wound offered an earthly sort of reassurance; both were a testament to the past that was getting harder and harder to hold on to.

He walked to the table. Opened the basket. Nested atop a bed of timothy grass and lavender sat a smooth ceramic bowl filled with broth and covered with plastic wrap. Two vent holes let the soup's steam and scent escape into the ether. Beside the bowl was a plate with a corn biscuit and a pat of butter, also covered in plastic wrap. Next to that sat a mug and a pot of hot tea that smelled of mint and honey.

Arman's stomach felt too jumpy to eat, but he knew who'd brought the food for him and it was knowledge that made him feel good. Cared for. He glanced out the cabin's window. The day's shadows had grown long. Everyone must still be down in the meeting hall. Dr. Gary had said they'd be there until dinner, which, if yesterday was anything to go by, wouldn't happen until well after dark.

That meant now might be a good time to visit the cook. For him to try to talk to her. Arman's body quivered at the thought, unable to resist indulging in the memory of her perfect touch, her open mouth, the sweet-soft way her breasts rubbed beneath that flimsy dress she wore, just barely a secret. It all had power to fill him with the most dizzying sort of agony. There could be nothing more earthly than that. Besides, she would listen to what he had to say. She would believe him. And she would know what to do.

Wouldn't she?

20

THERE WAS ONE THING ARMAN needed to do before heading down to the kitchen to see the cook: hide his money. Leaving it in the cabin seemed unwise with the way things were disappearing around the compound. But dragging his whole bag around with him everywhere also felt like a bad idea. Someone might ask what was in it. Worse, they might take the bag from him and look inside.

So Arman scooped the newspaper-wrapped bills from his bag, tucked the entire bulky bundle under his shirt, and left the cabin. After looking around to make sure no one was following him, he ducked into the woods, traveling as far west as he could on soft feet, quiet as a prey animal.

He skidded down a steep hill into a narrow ravine, following the path of a dry creek bed until he came upon a small hollow that was completely shaded and covered in ferns. Falling to his knees, Arman dug at the soft dirt beneath the plants until the hole was big enough. Then he dropped the money in, covered it up, and placed two flat stones over the top, followed by a handful of pine needles.

Arman stood. Wiped the dirt from his hands and sweat from his forehead. He didn't look back as he walked away from the fern hollow, toward the ring of cabins. He felt better now. Unburdened. No one had seen him come out here. He was sure of it. And he wouldn't forget this spot. When the time finally came for him to leave this place for good, once he'd found Beau and figured out what the hell had happened to him, Arman would remember right where this was.

He had no doubt about it.

I need something good this summer, Arman.

Something I care about.

Shoulders brushing aside thick sunflower stalks and tall ears of summer corn, Arman made his way through the kitchen's lush garden with the words Beau had spoken to him here, just yesterday, playing and replaying in his head. He passed the berry bushes, all heavy with fruit, and the feathery chicken coop, and he remembered Beau's pride. His eagerness to get *started* and the solemn way he'd wanted Arman to know that they were alike. That they saw the world the same way because of how they'd grown up. Although that couldn't be true, Arman realized now, because he didn't believe in suicide. In part, because it was a dramatic gesture he didn't think he deserved, but also because suicide was something selfish people did. People who couldn't be bothered to care about others.

Wasn't it?

Arman also couldn't help but think of last night. What he'd been urged to do with that knife. The dot of blood he'd drawn before stopping.

Had Beau *meant* for him to kill him?

Was that what he wanted?

Overhead, the sun sank from the sky in its arrogant, look-at-me way, but Arman kept his head down. He couldn't stomach seeing the light or pondering questions that might make him sick to answer. He focused on keeping his feet moving, and as he reached the kitchen's garden entrance at last, he found the sliding glass door open. Like an invitation.

Like she knew he was coming.

Arman began to walk faster, pulled in by a tide of anticipation. A wave of heat swept from his belly to his groin, stiffening him and heightening his senses almost to the point of actual pain.

Breathe, he told himself as he stepped into a kitchen that buzzed with energy. Then he stopped. And stared. Because everything was different. Unlike yesterday, when the cook had been the only one here, the room was now filled with workers, at least half a dozen of them, who were preparing for dinner service; roasting vegetables; taking trays of meat out of the oven; pouring carafes of ice water and wine; and yelling to each other about issues like place settings and the number of chairs and who was going to light the incense. Arman licked his lips. Where had all these people come from?

And where had they been yesterday?

The cook, however, wasn't among the workers. She wasn't anywhere. Arman looked all around before leaving the kitchen in confusion. He started to walk back across the garden. He planned to make his way around to the front of the building to the dining hall entrance, where he hoped to find her. He also hoped to tame some of his neediness in the meantime, to gain some semblance of control over the fire that raged between his legs. He really was in the worst sort of way.

Then he saw her.

She was in the vegetable beds, crouched by a standing trellis in the fading light. The lattice of the trellis was twined with what looked like snap peas, which the cook was picking, collecting them in a clear plastic bowl. She also held a set of shears stuck between her teeth, very gently, the way a Labrador might hold its duck. And maybe it was the intensity of her focus or the intensity of the day, but looking at her not only failed to diminish his sense of desire, it swelled and grew. It threatened to swallow him whole.

Arman walked over. Cleared his throat.

The cook jumped. She squinted up at him. Removed the shears from her mouth.

"Hey." He gave a small wave.

"What are you doing here?" she asked sharply.

"I came to see you."

"Me? Why?"

"I wanted to talk."

"Talk?"

He shrugged. "Yeah."

Her gaze darted behind him. "Well, did anyone see you?"

"See what?"

"Did anyone see you come over here? Did Mari see you? She was out here before. Checking on me."

Arman faltered. "Mari? No. I don't think so. Why?"

The cook gripped the bowl of snap peas to her chest. "You can't be here, you know. We can't be seen together."

"Why not?"

"It's against the rules."

"Whose rules?"

She glanced over her shoulder. "Look, I can't afford to get in trouble. And you can't either. Not everyone here likes you."

"They don't?"

She shook her head. "Beau wasn't supposed to bring you. Or your friends."

"My friends?"

"Those people you came with."

"They're not my friends."

"Sure seems like they are."

"But you were able to be with me yesterday."

The cook made a clucking sound, like Arman was a boy who'd done something wrong but who was still, at heart, mostly innocent. "This isn't yesterday. And you told me you were leaving."

"I did leave. Then I came back."

"I heard you were sick, by the way. I brought you soup while you were sleeping."

"I know you did. Thank you. But who said that? I'm not sick. I hit my head. I had to get stitches. That's why I—"

There was a loud sound then—a massive crack-boom that shook the earth, startling them both. The scent of gunpowder filled the air. A flock of swallows burst from the brush in a flutter of wings.

"What was *that*?" Arman breathed.

The cook's face went pale. She scrambled to her feet, dropping her bowl in the process. Peas scattered on the ground.

"That was the cannon," she said.

"There's a cannon?"

She nodded. "It means Inoculation's over. You have to go now. I do, too."

"But I need to talk." Arman took a step toward her. "Things have been happening to me. Things I don't understand."

The cook backed away. She held up her hands so that the kitchen shears were between them, glinting in the twilight. "Don't come any closer, Arman. I mean it. You *can't.*"

"*What?*"

"Look, we'll talk later. I promise. Just not now, okay?"

"But—"

"Just go," she whispered urgently, her eyes darting once again to somewhere behind him. "For *me.*"

21

ARMAN TURNED AND LEFT. He managed to hold down the sting of bile rising in his throat as he walked away from her. But just barely.

Not everyone here likes you.

Beau wasn't supposed to bring you.

Shoulders heavy, he retreated through the garden along the same route he'd come in on. His desire wasn't just dampened now; it'd been washed away. Swamped. Every trace of it gone.

All around him, evening settled. The crickets sang, the world went sooty, and there was something in the earthly gloom and the vastness of the sky that made Arman feel both skittish and weak. And more than a little sad.

It was loneliness, he decided, stuffing his hands into his pockets. That was the source of his sadness. At the moment he felt more alone than ever, because he'd actually dared to let himself need something. Or, more accurately, *someone*.

Arman shivered. He was trying hard not to feel sorry for himself, since from what he could figure, self-pity was the only thing worse than self-loathing. Veering left at the trailhead fork, he headed in the direction of the domed meeting hall. At least he could sit in there, he thought. At least he wouldn't be alone.

The building soon came into view. The wood doors were open and warm light spilled out. People, too. They were leaving, and Arman hurried forward. He was eager to join the group's journey, no matter where it might lead. And that was a feeling that was new to him, he realized, all new—seeking solace in the presence of others.

Arman slipped in with the migrating crowd. There was nothing to it. No one noticed his presence or asked where he'd been. And in a twist of irony, it turned out the whole group was heading right back toward the dining hall he'd just come from. Although they were walking to the front entrance, of course. Not the kitchen.

Entering the hall, with its dim light and heady atmosphere, Arman trailed near the back of the line with one hand over his stomach. He smelled the food coming from the kitchen, rich and savory, but he wasn't hungry. His sick feeling had grown exponentially since leaving the garden.

He collapsed in the first open chair he came to. The room had started to spin, and staying on his feet seemed risky. Maybe if he put his throbbing head down and closed his eyes, he'd wake up feeling better. More stable. Or better yet, maybe the world would be a different place. And he'd be a different person.

One with a life that made sense.

Four people were already seated at the table he'd chosen. Arman had no idea who they were, only that they were loud and in the middle of a heated debate. So much for sleeping. Their cynical tones and righteous indignation soured Arman's stomach more than it already was. Dinner-table tension never sat well with him.

"But it's the *principle* that matters," an owlish man with red flyaway hair and wire-rimmed glasses was saying, jabbing the air with his fork for emphasis. "Nothing else. We don't need to change what we're doing. We just need to be *right*. The Evolution will come about naturally. It will be a moral imperative."

"The principle is never what matters." A thin woman on his left corrected him. "Morality isn't how change happens. Humans define morality based on their actions. Not the other way around. We always reason to our advantage and we give ourselves all sorts of outs. Look at the doctrine of double effect. That's the very *essence* of what Haidt is talking about."

"Moral dumbfounding," agreed another woman. "Gary says it's the reason the younger generations are so dangerous right now. They believe their every urge is valid. They're not going to willingly give that up."

"Ridiculous," the first man huffed. "Moral relativism is a myth. Gary and Haidt can both say what they want, but at the end of the day it's like trying to compare the Bible with carbon dating or quantum physics. It doesn't hold up."

"So you're not in favor of Containment?" the first woman asked.

"I'm saying that from an epistemological perspective, we can't afford solipsism. Containment is a means to an end. Forget the double effect. Immunity's about the herd as much as the self."

And so it went.

Arman unfolded a napkin. Placed it in his lap. He had no clue what Containment was, or this double effect, but seeing as he was younger and all, did that mean these people actually thought *he* was dangerous? It would've been amusing if he didn't feel so awful. But the whole conversation was weird, and Arman suspected the already-near-empty wine carafe in the center of the table had a lot to do with it.

The food came soon after. Not the fragrant broth the cook had left for Arman back in the cabin. No, this meal was richer. Heavier. Far more decadent. There was brown-sugar-crusted pork loin stuffed with plums and bourbon-soaked figs. There were roasted turnips seasoned with herbs. Bright wraps of rainbow chard filled with goat cheese. Blackberry salsa. Small pots of butter.

When the cook stopped by his table, Arman knew better than to talk to her. It was against the rules. She'd told him that. But knowing didn't stop him. It never did.

"When can we meet?" he blurted as she set a loaf of warm bread in front of him. "I really need to talk to you."

The cook shot him a cool look in return, one that made him shut his mouth fast. Jesus. He shrank in his chair. But Arman's shame melted like snow in summer when she leaned forward, reached beneath the table, and briefly squeezed his leg before turning and leaving without saying a word.

When she was gone, he looked down. She'd dropped a scrap of paper in his lap. On it was written:

Midnight. My place. Come to the window.

He shoved the paper into his pocket while everyone around him began passing food. Pouring more wine.

"Not hungry?" the old man next to Arman asked, and other than Kira, he was the only black person Arman had seen so far at the compound. That seemed strange, although Arman couldn't have said why. The guy was also really old. As in shaky hands, shriveled skin, and bones that appeared to have gotten lost inside of him. Arman was surprised he'd survived the van ride out here, much less any of the more grueling activities.

"I don't feel very good," Arman told him.

"Food'll help. It always helps."

"It won't help if I throw up."

The old man chuckled.

"Is that funny?" Arman asked.

"It's that girl, isn't it?"

"What girl?"

"The one who brought the food," the old man said. "I saw you looking at her. You know, I was the same way when I was your age."

"What way is that?"

"Feeling sick around the pretty ones. That was how I knew I liked them. Love-shy, they call it."

"Love-shy?"

"Scared of girls. Or whoever it is you like."

"Oh."

"I got over it, though."

"You did?"

"Yup."

"How?"

"You gotta spend time with them. That's the secret. The sick feeling goes away once you get to know the person. Or maybe it doesn't go away so much as your brain starts to figure out that caring about someone is a good feeling instead of a bad one. Brains are smart like that, you know. They'll find the truth."

"Mmm," Arman said, although he wasn't sure this information applied to him. His concussion was the main reason he felt sick at the moment. Besides, he wasn't just love-shy. He was shy-shy. All the time. Around everything. And so far his dumb brain hadn't figured out how to do anything smart about it at all.

Arman took a sip of ice water. Saw the old man was still staring at him.

"How's the, uh, food?" he asked.

"You know, I think I recognize you," the old man said.

"You do?"

"Definitely."

"Well, I've been here since yesterday," Arman said. "So I guess that makes sense."

"No, that's not it. I know you from somewhere else."

"I don't know what to tell you."

The old man scrunched up his face. "Or maybe you just look like someone."

"Maybe I do."

"Where are you from anyway?"

"I thought you weren't supposed to ask me that."

"I just want to figure out where I know you from, kid. I don't need your autobiography."

"I'm from Santa Cruz," Arman said quickly. "You?"

"Oakland. Sat on the bench as a superior court judge there for twenty-five years."

"That's a long time."

"It is. It's actually how I first met Beauregard."

"You met him at the courthouse?"

"Yup."

"So he was a judge?"

"Definitely not. *I* wasn't even a judge back then. But when I met him, he was only eighteen."

"Oh."

"You know, I'm *sure* I recognize you."

Arman squirmed under the weight of the old man's gaze. He tried changing the subject by tipping his head toward the group on the other side of the table. Their discussion had grown even more heated, the debate having moved on from moral relativism to group dynamics and someone or something called a Bion.

"So what's that all about?" Arman asked.

"Bunch of idiots," muttered the old man.

"Yeah?"

"Absolutely. They should know better. Goddamn waste of time, arguing over all that philosophical crap. There's no point debating the nature of existence in a place like this. None."

"There's not?"

"Oh no. It's a sign of stagnation. That's what Wilfred Bion really said. Most people don't want to change. No matter what they say or the more they say it. I taught Beau that a long time ago. That if you aren't moving forward, you're falling toward irrelevancy. And talking's not moving, you know."

"But Beau wants to move forward?"

"Indeed. He gets pushback, though, from people like these fools, people who don't have his vision. They fear irrelevancy, but they want to be comfortable, so they tell themselves they're doing something important by doing nothing. Pure arrogance. Frighteningly so."

"Frightening?"

The old man nodded. Leaned closer. "Mark my words, son, when arrogance and fear are used to cover self-deception, that's the most dangerous sort of lie there is."

Dr. Gary walked over to Arman as the meal ended. Dishes were being cleared and people were starting to leave.

"Didn't think I'd see you here," he said, putting his hands on the back of Arman's chair. The old man beside Arman gave the doctor a startled look, then got up. Left without saying a word.

Arman stared after him. Wished he could leave, too. Dr. Gary reminded Arman of teachers he'd had back in elementary school, the ones who demanded nothing of him in terms of education or learning; only that he listen to their boring personal stories and not ask questions they didn't want to answer. Not to mention, Arman hated the way it felt to have someone looming over him. Like he was a mouse stuck between a cat's paws.

"I didn't want to miss anything," he said finally.

"Can I take that to mean you're still interested in us?" Dr. Gary asked. "In the things we have to teach?"

"I've always been interested. That's why I came here in the first place."

"But you also said you tried to leave this morning."

Arman twisted his neck to look up at him. "So you believe me now? About what happened?"

Dr. Gary squeezed his shoulder, then came around to sit in the chair the old man had vacated. "I only believe in what I have evidence of, Arman. That's the reason my faith points inward these days, much to the disappointment of my Baptist mother. But it's also why I believe you when you say you *wanted* to leave."

Um, was that sentiment meant to be reassuring? Arman thought it was about the most patronizing thing he'd heard in a while. Like telling a kid you believed he *wanted* to win a race when he'd come in dead last. Like he didn't already know he was a loser.

"I was scared," he said after a moment. "That's why I left. I wanted to be here, but I didn't think I deserved to be."

"And now?"

Arman racked his brain for the most noncommittal answer. "Now I want to try. I want to get better."

The doctor smiled. "I'm glad to hear it. Tell me, did you sleep? Your brain can't heal without it."

"A little bit."

"How do you feel now?"

"I still have a headache. And my stomach kind of hurts. I can't eat."

"Your stomach?"

"Yeah."

"Well, here." Dr. Gary produced a bottle of pills from a leather bag he carried. "Take two more of these painkillers, and I'll go get you some ginger tea and plain toast from the kitchen. That'll help your stomach, okay?"

"Okay." Arman fumbled with the lid for a moment, shook the pills out, then went to hand the bottle back.

"Keep it," Dr. Gary said. "That way you can take them as needed."

Arman shrugged and slid the bottle into his shirt pocket. He pointed at the dwindling crowd as they trickled from the dining room to go who knew where. "Tonight's not another long hike in the dark is it?"

"Long? No. Tonight's Vespers."

"What's Vespers?"

"Oh, I think you'll like it."

"Do I have to go?"

"You said you didn't want to miss anything."

That felt less like an answer and more like a threat.

"When's Containment?" he asked impulsively.

Dr. Gary cocked his head. "Where did you hear about Containment? Did Virgil say something?"

Arman hedged. "I think someone mentioned it at dinner."

"I bet they did. Well, focus on tonight. You understand? When you're done with your tea, just walk up to the meadow. You'll find us. We start in ten minutes."

"Okay."

"One more thing, Arman," Dr. Gary said.

"What is it?"

"Don't be late."

22

BY THE TIME ARMAN DRAINED the last of his tea, he was starting to feel better. His stomach calmed, and the pulse of pain inside his skull eased to a faint throbbing. He was alone in the dining hall by this point, so he picked up his empty mug and plate full of crumbs. Walked back toward the kitchen and slowly opened the swinging door.

He poked his head in. Much to his disappointment, the cook wasn't there. Instead he found the same workers from earlier still buzzing around. They were washing dishes, wiping down counters.

"Where should I put these?" he asked, holding up the mug and plate.

One of the workers pointed at the counter. Arman set the items down. And left.

Arriving in the meadow, where Dr. Gary had told him to go, Arman stared in disbelief. The entire field had been transformed. In the very center stood a giant white tent. Gauzy and ethereal, with long strands of twinkling amber globes lining the structure both inside and out, there was a warmth to the sight that Arman found appealing. Nostalgic with a hint of formality. It reminded him of a wedding. Or an inauguration.

Or some other sort of ceremony.

He walked to the tent's entrance. The flaps were pulled back and knotted with ivy. Baskets of wildflowers and loose petals lined the dirt path leading inward and it was as if he were meant to imagine the tent had sprouted from the earth, wholly organic. Music poured from beneath the looming canopy, something frenetic and dissonant yet utterly enthralling. It plucked his nerves and filled Arman with the most dire sense of longing.

"What are you waiting for?" a voice asked.

Arman turned his head. The dark-haired woman stood in the shadows, just a few feet away, and she watched him, arms folded. There were small lines etched around her eyes and at the corners of her mouth. As if the mere sight of him was making her crack.

"I'm not waiting for anything," he replied.

"Aren't you, though?" She took a step toward him. "You don't fool me, Arman."

"I don't?"

"I know how you got here. I know what you did. But you're not going to get what you came for."

"What did I come here for?"

She kept her steely gaze on him. "Everyone has to earn what they've been given. It's one of our basic principles."

"Yeah, okay," he said, before ducking into the tent and scooting away from her scowling face.

Inside, people were seated on creaking rows of wood benches, all facing the back wall. That was where an empty lectern stood, flanked by more baskets of flowers and a burning candelabra. Everything smelled strongly of incense.

Everything felt gravely important.

Normally, walking through a crowded space and having to find a spot to insert himself was the type of activity that made Arman's hands sweat and his throat close up. But the pills he'd taken dulled his anxiety to the point where he was able to stroll the tent, searching for an empty seat without wanting to bolt. It was as if his tendency to overthink had been tied up and shoved away in some remote part of his brain; it was still there, but it wasn't controlling him. Not completely.

After a moment, Arman spied Kira's long braids on the end of a bench about two-thirds of the way toward the back and made his way over.

"Hey," he said softly, squeezing past people to settle beside her. His body tingled at their closeness, at the way his arm brushed against hers.

"Oh, hey," she said. Then she wrinkled her nose: "You smell funny."

"What do I smell like?"

"Like booze," she said. "Or barf."

At this Arman laughed. He couldn't help himself. "Thank you. That's very flattering."

"What happened to your head?"

"It's a long story."

"You haven't seen Dale around, have you?"

"Not since before dinner."

Kira glanced over her shoulder. Chewed a fingernail. "He'd better not be late."

Arman shrugged. In his mind, that train had already left the station; the tent's flaps were being unknotted—the lights dimmed, the music turned down. Whatever was going to happen was happening now.

But then there he was.

Dale poked his head through the tent's entrance and tried walking in, only he was stopped by someone. Arman strained to look. Was it that Brian guy, the one who'd been a dick to him earlier? He couldn't tell, but whoever it was gave Dale a hard time. His face went all red and he raised his voice. Then the person talking to him put a hand on his chest. Pushed him out of the tent.

Arman stared at Kira. "What was that all about?"

"Shh!" she said.

"Well, aren't you going to help him?"

She pinched his arm. "Shut it, already. Otherwise that bitch is going to yell at us."

What bitch? The dark-haired woman? Arman snapped around to face forward and sat up straight. He definitely didn't want to deal with *her*.

But when he looked, it was Mari who'd stepped up to the lectern.

SO LONG TO ANSWER.

The girl is the first to finish answering your questionnaire. She walks over and hands it to you with an air of accomplishment. A breathless pause. She's completed a task for you, and she wants you to tell her that she's good enough.

You will, of course. But that's not to say you always do. You have standards and you make it a point to stick to them. No one who's too pushy, too sappy, too righteous, too horny. These are qualities you don't like.

These are people you can't sway.

The girl sits across from you. She's eager because she's sure of herself. But you take your time. You look carefully at her answers. This is in part for show, but it's also because you're interested. What she's written down is what she wants you to know.

You find yourself wanting to listen.

By the answers she's marked, she's telling you a lot of things, all at once: that she can't sleep, she can't eat, that she's lost purpose in life. And you know that what she's really saying is "I'm depressed," and "I want help."

But there are others things she's saying. There are deeper truths that you hear.

Truths like:

"I'm tired."

"I'm hungry."

"I want you to nourish me."

And this, this, is what you've been waiting for. These are the needs you knew she had.

These are the truths you so long to answer.

23

"GOOD EVENING," MARI SAID TO the crowd.

"Good evening," everyone said back.

"I hope you're all proud of the work you did today. I know it wasn't easy, but change never is. It's why only the strong ever do it. It's why we're proud of you, too."

Arman shifted in his seat. He hadn't done any of the work she was talking about. In fact, he'd purposely tried to run away so that he wouldn't *have* to do it, a fact that didn't make him feel very strong or proud.

"Tonight," Mari continued, "is Vespers, which is the time we'll take to pause and reflect on one of the most powerful emotions in human experience. We're going to explore the ways in which it can impact our sense of the world, our sense of others, and of ourselves, as well as the ways we can control it, rather than being controlled. Do you understand?"

Everyone nodded. Arman included.

"Good. But before we begin, I want you to take a look at who's sitting next to you."

Kira looked at Arman, and Arman looked at her.

"Now ask yourself, did you know this person from before you came here? Do they know anything about your Before Life and the person you were then? If so, I'd like for you to stand up and switch seats." Mari paused. "Do it. Right now. The strongest bonds are the ones we build together."

Arman gazed at Kira with a hypnotic dreaminess. What did he *really* know about her? He knew she was hot in ways that could make him feel uncomfortable. That she was smart in ways that could make him feel hopeless. That her father not wanting her to date Dale had been enough to drive her here, but that she must care for her father enough that his opinion mattered to her in the first place. That was it.

He didn't know much about her at all.

But Kira hopped up to move. Before Arman had a chance to ask her to stay. He didn't mind, though. He watched her go the way a stone might watch the rain come down, which was to say with a deep sense of fatalism.

A few other people shifted around as well. And Dale had returned. Arman spotted him sitting hunched in the very last row with a dark expression on his face. Arman couldn't imagine what the penalty was for being late, but it didn't look good.

When the moving was done, Mari picked the microphone back up. Cleared her throat.

"Close your eyes," she told them.

"Now I want you to think back to a time in your life, anytime, it could be recent, it could be from your childhood, whatever comes to mind. But I want you to think of a time when you felt *ashamed*. Not embarrassed. Or self-conscious. Or regretful. But ashamed. That's the emotion you need to tap into right now. And remember, we talked about this earlier, shame comes from the outside. From others. That's what makes it toxic. Insidiously so. It's designed to trick you, to suppress your natural process of self-evaluation. The sole purpose of shame is to make you submit to the will of others.

"Once you have your moment, I want you to go over every detail of this event. Replay it in your mind's eye, like you're watching a movie. Try to remember *everything* that was happening at the time. Use all your senses. Taste. Smell. Touch. And while you're doing this, I want you to pinpoint the precise moment you felt the shame. I want you to remember exactly what it was you were doing and whose judgment you were internalizing."

Arman took a deep breath. The moment that sprang to his mind was surprising only in that he didn't reject it outright and choose something easier. But Arman did what he was instructed to.

He remembered.

Everything.

He was fourteen when it happened. He'd been sent to stay with his father and his father's parents up in Marin for the entire week of Thanksgiving break. Even after he'd asked not to go. Even after he'd begged. But his mother made such a stink, Arman suspected his grandparents had paid her off. Or else she'd paid them.

And it wasn't that he didn't like his grandparents. The elder Dukoffs were nice enough, in the way nice strangers could be. They sent him cards for his birthday and sometimes money. But Arman wasn't going for them. He was going for his father, who was fresh out of prison on drug charges. And he wasn't going because his dad wanted to see him or anything but because his grandparents thought Arman could fix his father.

He couldn't, of course. But he was forced to endure hours alone with his dad, who skipped out on his NA meetings every day to sit in the garden of his parents' enormous hillside house and chain-smoke.

"We're going to make a man out of you," he'd tell Arman, with his mirrored sunglasses on and his legs kicked up on the glass-topped table. "But not here. Not in the States. See, I got this friend in Belize who's developing a resort. He's going to let me buy in early. Maybe even get that jazz club going like I've been wanting." Arman's dad would glance over at him while he spoke, to make sure Arman was listening. "You and I, we'll go down there together, okay? You'll love it. I know you will. I'll teach you how to drink. The girls there'll teach you how to fuck. It's going to be good for us, kid. It's not going to be like before. I promise."

"B-but don't you need money for all that?" Arman would squeak as he fidgeted with the landscaping, picking at the prettiest flowers and throwing them into the koi pond. Everything smelled like honey. "Like a real job?"

"Shit, I got money, kid." He'd gesture toward the house. "I just need more time."

Arman knew what that meant. His dad thought he could sweet-talk his parents into giving him what he wanted, but even Arman knew that wasn't going to happen. No way. His parents were the two people on earth his dad couldn't con. Not anymore. So Arman had spent that whole week on edge, jittery, unable to sleep, with all the food he ate running through him and the length of his arms growing increasingly scabbed and bloody—a topographical map of dread—while he waited for the inevitable family blowup.

Only it didn't happen.

Instead, Arman bolted a day early, abandoning his father and his cigarettes and his stupid Belize dreams in that beautiful backyard beneath the autumn sun. He didn't even say good-bye. He just got on a bus and went home to his mother, who picked him up at the Santa Cruz station. Arman, who hadn't slept in three days and was ten pounds lighter than when he'd left, said nothing when he saw her. And he'd said nothing when she held his stiff shoulders and looked him in the eye and told him that in the mere two hours since Arman's departure, his dad had managed to OD on Crown Royal and stolen oxy and was in the hospital getting his stomach pumped.

But Arman said nothing at the news because he *felt* nothing. Just a hollow breeze through the hole where his emotions usually roiled. In fact, he was still numb later that evening, when he went into his room to change for bed. That was when he'd stood in his boxers by the window with an ancient Swiss Army knife gripped in one hand and the chill of the California night brushing against his skin. And fourteen-year-old Arman wasn't *angry* or *afraid* or *remorseful* as he dragged the blade across his thighs, back and forth and back again. He wasn't any of those things. He was nothing.

The way he always was.

But now, sitting on the wood bench in the tent with his eyes shut tight, Arman felt sad for himself, but embarrassed, too. Because like the scars on his legs, the *shame* had come afterward: telling his mom when the bleeding wouldn't stop. Telling the doctors at the hospital how he'd done it and why. Telling the therapist they made him see why he wouldn't do it again.

So there. That was it. *That's* what he'd been doing when he felt shame. It wasn't when he'd heard about what his useless dad had gone and done. It wasn't even when he'd hurt himself. It was when other people saw him for who he really was.

His father's son.

"Open your eyes," Mari said.

So he did.

"Now I want you to find someone close to you. Anyone. And I want you two to sit facing each other."

The seat next to Arman was still empty—no one had claimed Kira's spot. Fortunately, the person in front of him turned around. He was a young guy, younger than most around here, with messy brown hair and a navy hooded sweatshirt from UC Berkeley. He raised his bushy eyebrows at Arman as if to ask, *Us?*

Arman nodded. The guy wasn't anybody he knew or recognized, which he supposed was the point. He also looked as nervous as Arman felt—a little sweaty, a little sick. The guy swiveled his body around on the bench so that they sat facing each other.

"Now I want you and your partner to look each other in the eye," Mari directed. "You're going to keep that eye contact no matter what happens. And while you're doing this, I want you to notice what it is you're thinking and what you're feeling, and how those two connect."

Arman looked up and he met his partner's gaze. He knew doing so would make him feel awkward and it did. But he wasn't sure whether the awkwardness stemmed from looking so intently at someone who could see him looking. Or if it came from being seen.

But he kept looking.

And looking.

Until he saw something *strange*.

At first glance, Arman had thought the other guy's eyes were brown. Like his. Only where Arman's were muddy, bland, and forgettable, this guy's eyes were the palest color. Like sand stirred at the bottom of a shady stream. But the longer Arman looked at them, the more the color of his eyes changed, shifting from brown to gray, then brown again. Like river pebbles, Arman realized with a start.

He was looking at *Beau's* eyes.

That's impossible.

Arman felt a sway of dizziness.

(*Notice your feelings.*

Notice your thoughts.)

Well, that's what he was *trying* to do, but focusing on his own thoughts and feelings grew more difficult the more he stared at those familiar eyes.

What were *they* seeing?

And what, pray tell, were they feeling?

Oh, Beau, Arman thought desperately. *I don't know what happened. I don't know what to believe.*

Mari's voice cut in then, rolling with her lullaby prosody. "Very good. You're all doing a wonderful job. Now, without breaking eye contact, you're going to tell your partner three things about yourself that no one else knows. Three secrets. Real secrets. No censoring. No commenting. Just courage and commitment. Go."

Arman hesitated. This was worse than what he'd had to do up on Echo Rock. After all, secrets were secrets for a reason.

But you can do it, he told himself. *Do it for Beau. You owe him that.*

"I think I'm crazy," he said in an untamed rush. "Like, actually crazy."

"I ran away from home," the other guy said simultaneously.

They paused only for a beat. To take a breath, eyes still locked.

Then:

"I wish my father were dead."

"I hit my mom once."

And finally:

"You look like someone I know."

"I tried to kill myself," the guy with the river-pebble eyes told him. "I used a knife to cut my wrists and bled out. I nearly died."

24

ARMAN BROKE EYE CONTACT FIRST. He couldn't help it. The back of his neck tingled and he glanced away. But then he looked right back at the stranger sitting in front of him. "You *what*?"

"No commenting." Arman jumped because Mari was standing right behind him

"Sorry," he said.

She nodded but when she turned around again and wandered off, Arman leaned forward and hissed, "Did you say you tried to *kill* yourself? With a knife?"

The guy with the river-pebble eyes nodded. "But I was lucky. A friend found me in time. Took me to the ER."

Arman's mind crackled with anger. "Did someone put you up to this? It's not funny, you know. It's really fucking not funny."

The guy looked hurt. "I'm not like that anymore. This place, it's helped me. It's changed who I am. I know what the future has in store for me. Bright things. Wondrous things."

Now Arman was openly staring. "*What* did you just say?"

"Quiet," Mari said, looking pointedly at him from across the tent.

Arman bit his tongue.

"I want you all to close your eyes again," she began, shifting once more into her lulling voice, telling them to get comfortable, to loosen their muscles and loosen their minds, as she led them into more reflection, asking them to go deeper and connect the feelings between one exercise with those from the other. Arman tried following along, but his brain wouldn't settle. Some things in life just *couldn't* be a coincidence.

Could they?

Mari continued talking, asking the group to imagine walking through a field of flowers, warmed by sunlight that kissed their skin, and coming across a younger version of themselves. In their minds they were supposed to tell the child they found what they had learned that night and what they felt that child needed to know in order to be inoculated from shame for the future ahead of them.

Arman saw the boy inside his mind. The kid he'd been—fearful, worried, but occasionally callous. The spaced-out kid with the messy hair and cheap clothes, who got everything wrong and refused to try anymore, far preferring ignorance to failure. The achingly lonely kid with a bad habit of sulking on the basketball sidelines over never being picked to play, but who always said no if asked. Arman stared at that boy now, at his shuffling feet and sullen gaze, and he knew what he was meant to tell him:

Shame can't rule your life. It's okay to fail. It's okay to let people see you in pain. Pain and failure mean you're alive. But suppressing who you are, running away from your problems, those are just ways of letting other people live your life for you. Don't let them take that. Define yourself.

And maybe that's what he would've said if he were like the older people at the compound. If he were closer to death and relatively comfortable. If he really didn't want to deal with change that might challenge him. But he wasn't like that. Or he didn't want to be. His failures were his to own, and no amount of blame was going to change that. So when Arman opened his mouth, the words that came out were anything but brave or inspiring. No, instead of platitudes he couldn't persuade himself to believe, he told his younger self a rambling truth:

"Crazy things are going to happen to you, kid. They're going to happen and you aren't going to understand them and you aren't going to know how to deal. I'm telling you this now, so that maybe you'll be better off by the time you're my age. So that maybe you'll know what to do when nothing in the world makes any fucking sense, because I sure as hell don't. I'm telling you all this because I'm desperate. I'm telling you this so that when you're older maybe *you* can save *me*. Because you know what? No one else is going to."

Sometime later, Arman's eyes fluttered open. He was still seated on the wooden bench with his head slumped over. The music above him still played and the amber lights still glowed, but when he looked around, everyone was gone.

He was all alone.

Arman scrambled to his feet. He must've dozed off from those pills he'd taken. Well, that wasn't very impressive. How could he expect to control his response to social disease if he couldn't even keep his *eyes* open? He headed toward the exit, moving as fast as he could, but his headache was back, and his left leg had fallen asleep, giving him a prickly limp and making him swear.

Ducking beneath the tent flaps and stepping out into the night, Arman breathed a sigh of relief. Down the hillside, a huge bonfire roared, and the whole group, it seemed, had migrated toward the flames—everyone was either standing or sitting in chairs or on blankets spread out on the ground.

Arman hobbled over.

There was a weirdness surrounding the bonfire atmosphere. A catharsis, of sorts. Or a frenzy. Everywhere he turned, people were in states of extreme emotion. Uncomfortably so. Making his way around the clearing, Arman came upon a group of older men with their heads thrown back, laughing uproariously. He saw two women weeping and clinging to each other, then another two furiously making out. On the far side of the fire, lit by dancing flames, a different group was shouting and shoving at one another, seemingly on the verge of violence.

Catching sight of Kira and Dale seated on the ground in the grass, Arman hurried over to them.

"Hey," he said.

Kira looked up, but Dale didn't. He had his face pressed against Kira's chest and his arms curled tight against his stomach like a child, and his shoulders were shaking. Arman couldn't help but stare. What was going on? Was he *crying*?

"What is it?" Kira asked.

Arman swallowed. "Is he okay?"

"Not really."

"What's wrong?"

"He's having a hard time."

"Well, have you seen the guy I was paired up with in there?"

"What guy? In where?"

"In the tent."

"Oh, that," Kira said. "No, I didn't see who you were with."

"He was young. Maybe my height? He had a UC Berkeley sweatshirt on. And he—"

"Arman." She glanced down at Dale, who'd curled into an even tighter ball. Like a weepy armadillo. "I'm kind of busy right now."

"Sorry." Chagrined, Arman turned on his heel and left. He'd have to search for the guy with the river-pebble eyes on his own. Only after walking around and around, Arman couldn't find him anywhere. He did, however, find Mari. She stood next to the flames, very close. On his third lap around the fire, Arman walked over to her shyly.

"Hello, Arman," she said, without taking her eyes off the burning wood. "How are you feeling? How's your head?"

"My head's okay, I guess. Did I fall asleep in there?"

"Did it feel like you fell asleep?"

"It didn't feel like *anything*. The last thing I remember, you were leading us through some sunlit field so that we could talk to ourselves as children. The next thing I know, I'm alone in there."

"Then it sounds like you got what you needed."

"But why didn't anyone wake me up?"

"No one woke you up because your journey is yours alone to define. Also, you've had a long day. We thought you could use the rest."

Arman couldn't really argue with that. "Well, have you seen the guy I was paired with? With the UC Berkeley sweatshirt?"

"What guy?"

"He was sitting right in front me. He had brown hair. We did the eye contact thing."

"I didn't see you with a guy. I thought you were with . . ."

"With who?"

"That girl with the braids."

"Kira? She moved. You told us not to sit by people we knew."

"Ah."

"But you do know who I'm talking about, right? The guy with the sweatshirt?"

She shook her head. "I'm sorry. I have no idea who that is. Why?"

"Because I need to find him. I need to ask him about something he said. It's kind of important."

Mari smiled. "No commenting, remember?"

"I *know*. It's just, some of the things he said to me. They—"

"They what?"

"Well, they reminded me of Beau," Arman said. "He said things that Beau said to me today. Things no one else could know."

"I'm afraid I don't understand."

"Me neither! That's why I need to find him."

Mari reached a warm hand out. Touched his cheek.

"Arman," she said, with far more tenderness than he deserved.

His throat went thick. It took a moment before he could talk, and even then, his voice wavered. "Look, I *know* what you're going to say. That I'm hurt. And confused. And you're right, maybe I am. But I also know what I saw, okay? I don't care that it doesn't make sense and I don't care that no one believes me."

"I believe *in* you," Mari said. "More than you know. But I also believe that changing oneself is a difficult process. A painful one. More so for some than for others. And maybe you're not supposed to understand everything that's happening to you right now. Maybe it's the you who you'll become who will be able to make sense of it all."

Arman stared at the ground. "Yeah. Maybe. I guess."

"Are you all right?"

He gave a quick nod. "Can I ask you something?"

"Of course."

"That doctor guy. The one who did my stitches . . ."

"What about him?"

"He was talking about closing this place. Sealing it off so no one could get in or out. Making it sterile or something."

"You heard him say this?"

"Yes."

"Okay."

"Well, is that really what Beau wants?"

Mari sighed. "I don't know all of Beau's wants. Or Gary's for that matter. But I do know that Gary says a lot of things that aren't always worth listening to. Some of his ideas are . . ."

"Are what?"

She paused. "You know, never mind. It's not important. Why are you so interested, anyway?"

Arman's nostrils flared. He wanted her to trust him. "I don't know. It's just, Beau told me something. Yesterday, actually. And I thought—"

"What did he tell you?"

"He said there was someone here who wanted to ruin what he'd built."

"And you think he meant Gary?"

"I don't know what to think! But I probably shouldn't be talking about this, right? I mean, I'm crazy. Like really crazy. I'm not worth listening to."

"You're absolutely worth listening to," Mari said. "And you're not crazy. Whatever happened to you today has meaning. Above all else, I can promise you that. And your emotions are so close to the surface, you might almost be there."

"Be where?"

"On the verge of your breakthrough."

"You think?"

She smiled. "That's for you to think about. Not me."

Of course. Arman's cheeks went hot. "Do you know what time it is?"

"It's almost midnight."

Midnight. "Do I have to stay?"

"Do you want to go?"

"Yes. I think so. I do."

"Then go," she said. "That's your choice. When you're here, you're always free to go."

25

AND THEN HE WAS WITH the cook. They were in the shadows. In her room. In her narrow bed. They lay facing each other with their heads on the thin sheets, and the moonlight drifting through the window he'd crawled through to get to her. She reached to touch his forehead, near his injury, and more than anything, Arman wanted to lose himself with her, be lost, be anyone but who he was in that moment. But he couldn't get his mind to stop spinning.

"How did it happen?" she asked, slowly sliding her fingers from his stitches to his chin. Slowly setting a fire loose inside of him.

"I don't know," he said. "I can't remember."

"You can't remember?"

"No."

"That must be a strange feeling. Not knowing how you were hurt."

"It is." Arman ached for her to stroke him more.

"Poor you."

He rested his cheek on her arm. Relished the way his eyelashes brushed against her skin. "It wasn't easy getting here tonight, you know. It took forever. After what you said about the rules, I wanted to make sure no one saw me."

She gave a grin. "A real hero's journey, huh?"

"I suppose."

"How'd you do it?"

"I came up through the woods. Then I had to walk all the way around that old building and down into the gully. It was steep, too. And muddy. My shoes got wet. I left them outside."

"What old building?"

"That square one. Where the doctor's office is. There was a light on in there. On the second floor."

"What doctor's office?"

"You don't know where it is?"

"I didn't know one existed. Who's this doctor?"

"Gary. He's one of the trainers. Short, silver hair. Kind of paunchy."

"Oh." She wrinkled her nose. "I know who you're talking about. Look, stay away from him, okay? All of them."

"All of who?"

"Those trainers. The three of them."

"Why?"

"Because I don't trust them. Beau doesn't either."

Arman propped himself up on his elbow. "He doesn't?"

"No."

"Do you mean Mari, too? I like Mari."

The cook snorted. "*She's* the worst of all. She hates me. She's been trying to get me fired for ages."

"Really?"

She nodded. "I think they're the ones who got Beau called away this morning."

"Why would they do that?"

"To get people on their side."

"But I thought it was just Gary who wanted to close the compound.

Keep the place isolated. Or uncontaminated. Or whatever."

"Maybe it is," she said. "I don't know. I told you I don't like any of them."

"But you all work for Beau, don't you?"

"No one works *for* anybody. That's the whole idea. Everyone's here because they want to be. When Beau first bought this property, he'd already been running weekend workshops up in the Bay Area. But he wanted a space that was dedicated to healing. Where he could do more intense work. People responded by staying here longer and longer, wanting to be a part of what he was creating. Beau was fine with that, but we had to work. Pay our way. Help keep this place running so that he could go out and make a difference in the world. It was good. Really good. And everything was fine until last January."

"What happened last January?"

She sighed.

"What?"

"That's when Beau had to leave us for a little while. Not long. Just a few months, but it was enough time for things to . . . change. And not in a good way."

"What do you mean?"

"It's complicated."

"You and Beau are pretty close," he said. "Aren't you?"

"He's everything to me."

There was something about those words and the way she said them that didn't sit well with Arman; it also made his courage wither. If she cared so much about the man she'd dedicated her life to, then he didn't know how to tell her he was dead. That he'd killed himself.

So he decided not to say anything.

"So what happened to you today?" she asked. "After you left?"

"I don't know."

"What do you mean you don't know? Did you forget that, too?"

"I mean something happened to me that couldn't have. And no one believes me."

"I believe you," she said quickly.

"But you don't even know what happened."

"I don't need to know."

"Then how can you know it's true?"

"I didn't say it was *true*. I said I believed you. There's a difference, you know."

Arman felt flustered. Hadn't Beau said something similar to him? That the truth could be a lie. "But how can you believe something that isn't true?"

"Well, *you* do, don't you? You just told me you did. And I believe you. There's just something believable about you. I saw it the first time we met."

"You did?"

She nodded.

He gave a sigh. "But impossible things *keep* happening."

"Like what?"

"Like tonight. During Vespers, I could've sworn I saw—"

"You saw what?"

"A ghost," he whispered.

"Then I believe that, too," she said.

Later.

Under the cover of darkness, the cook did all the things to Arman that he wanted her to do but didn't know how to say. Or ask for. Or even fantasize about. And there was a magic to it all, he found, in the way acts so glaringly obvious could be so brilliantly singular.

But the cook also did things that set off his worrying, fears bright and unbidden. Of course, it was possible his worrying had nothing to do with her and everything to do with him, seeing as Arman was pretty sure the needle on his anxiety meter had been cranked past HIGH DECI-BEL WORRYING into the realm of madness ever since he'd stepped off the compound property that morning.

It was also possible that this was how he was *supposed* to feel when he was naked and with a girl and filled with so much heat. After all, he would do *anything* to have her.

Wouldn't he?

just ask just ask just ask just ask her already

But asking was easier said than done. Always. So it wasn't until she was already on top of him and he was already lost inside of her, that Arman gathered the nerve to pause, grip her soft waist, and whisper, "Shouldn't we be using something . . . doing something to . . . I mean, you know?"

"What do you think?" she asked with a sly smile on her lips, not bothering to pause at all.

He nodded. "I think . . . I think we should."

"So what are you going to do about it?"

Only it turned out what he was doing right then made the question inconsequential. Or hypothetical, really. He couldn't help it and he hated himself for that, even though he loved the way it felt. And after, when she'd rolled off him and rolled over, Arman remained unsettled. Distressingly so, with the relentless purr of regret rumbling through his mind.

stupid that was so stupid of me

Arman clasped his hands over his ears. Tried to drown out his worries. Maybe he should stop thinking altogether. Maybe that was the answer. It's what Beau told him to do, right? After all, when Arman was with the cook, he felt wanted. Needed. Wasn't that what mattered? Wasn't that the only thing?

But, his traitorous brain couldn't help but wonder, *if her wanting always takes things from me, am I really needed?*

Or am I being used?

THE DESTINY OF OTHER MEN.

As strange as it sounds, your own origin story is easy enough to imagine. And while it's not something you choose to talk about—you don't tell the girl and you don't invite questions about yourself—it's a story that's important. It's the stuff legends are made of. Almost too unbelievable to be true. But fantastic enough to have faith in.

You picture it happening like this: A man, a good man and a wise man, is put in jail for some small infraction. A misinterpretation of the law. An ungenerous act. You're not sure about the details, but details are where the devil lies in wait, so it's not like you look too closely.

This wise man is patient about his situation. It will take time to unravel, but he'll land on his feet. He always does. And he's wise enough to recognize this time as an opportunity for self-reflection. To think about his own weaknesses. His frailties. His power isn't what it used to be. He lacks shine, if not vision, and for the most part, only a certain type of person is drawn to look beneath his surface anymore. Only they aren't the people he needs to keep growing. It would be easy to convince himself otherwise, but self-deception's the only kind that's never gotten him anywhere.

While he waits for salvation in the form of a man of the law who saved him so many years ago, he makes the most of his current situation. Which is to say, he listens more than he talks. There's a lot to listen to; the man he's locked up with likes to talk and talk and talk.

This talking man's a sad one. He's lost hope and for good reason; every opportunity he's had—and he's had a lot—has been squandered. Or smoked. Or thrown away. He won't be saved anytime soon and there's nothing left to take away his pain. He speaks of his regrets as if confessing his sins. Worse even, as if he believes confessing might help.

The wise man knows it won't help. He knows that shifting one's belief system in the face of hopelessness is the most foolish sort of thinking. But that doesn't stop him from listening and listening well.

After all, one man's hopelessness can so often be another man's destiny.

26

ARMAN LAY IN THE DARK with his eyes open, with his chest rattling. Listening. He waited until the cook was in a deep sleep, her breathing slow, heavy, and hot against his back. Then he slipped from under her arm and out of her bed. He found his clothes. Dressed. Crept to the window. It opened easily. He slid out feetfirst, letting himself drop the last foot or so to land in the soft dirt. That's where his damp shoes were. He sat on the ground to put them on, then glanced into the woods around him.

His shoulders drooped to see the darkness. To see nothing. There was a part of Arman, bruised and sad, that didn't want to walk back to his cabin and face reality. But he didn't want to stay here, either. Or go anywhere else in the world. He simply wanted to crawl beneath a tree, curl in a bed of pine needles, and vanish. But he didn't do that. A lack of courage, perhaps, or a lack of faith in his ability to ever finish what he started. Instead he picked at his arm until the feeling passed, which meant there was blood.

And pain.

Eventually Arman got to his feet and began moving. He didn't know where he was going, but he marched with purpose, walking until he'd passed the meadow, where there was no sign of any bonfire, the domed building, which was now dark and still, and the spot where he'd left the van, which of course wasn't there and maybe never had been.

Finally, he reached the far boundaries of his existence: the iron gate.

Arman wasn't ready to leave, not yet, but it occurred to him that he could slip from the compound and check something. Just for the briefest second. He remembered the way the van's tires had squealed as he'd turned up the drive. Surely that would have left burn marks on the asphalt. Surely seeing those would prove the van had actually been here and that he wasn't crazy.

So he *had* to look.

The gate was locked. The heavy chain was wrapped around both sides, padlock dangling from the center. Arman walked up. Gripped his hands around the metal bars. He intended to climb over as he'd planned to before, although the task was more daunting now that he was actually facing it. He gazed up at the top of the fence, which appeared to be a good twenty-five feet high and lined with spikes. Arman prayed he wouldn't get impaled for his effort. There was no harness or rope, this time. No one to coach him from below.

Placing a foot on one of the decorative scrolls, Arman braced himself, then leapt, catching his other foot on a hold above the first. From there he pulled himself up with a groan, straining with each arm to reach above his head.

He made it to the top like that—slowly picking his way up the scrolls. Swinging his leg over was a dicier move, involving a lot of grappling and cursing, but he managed to do it without compromising his reproductive system in any way, thank God. Arman shifted his arms and tried lowering himself to the bottom, but he slipped halfway down, leaving himself dangling ten feet in the air. His shoes scrabbled for support but found nothing. *Shit.* He had no choice. He closed his eyes and let go, dropping to the ground with a thud.

For a moment, Arman lay stunned. He didn't move. The fall not only wrenched his spine, it jolted his wounded head—a harsh reminder that pain could be sharp and jarring, not just smothering. He squeezed his eyes shut and waited until the worst had passed. Then, when he was able, he crawled to his feet and staggered down the long drive to the main road. It wasn't easy to make out in the moonlight, but after walking in circles, he found what he was looking for: fresh rubber marks scorched into the asphalt, not yet faded by dust or time or sun.

Arman breathed a long sigh of relief. Well, he wasn't *totally* crazy. He had proof of that now. The van had been here, and its subsequent disappearance meant someone was screwing with him. Or Beau. Or both of them.

That's when he heard it. From somewhere behind Arman came a gruff voice asking, "Just what the hell do you think you're doing?"

27

ARMAN TURNED AROUND. FELT HIS hackles rise. Sure enough, it was Brian. Stupid Brian.

"What do *you* want?" he sniped back.

Brian ignored him. Instead he pulled a military-looking walkie-talkie from under his weird clothes. Apparently the guy *did* have a holster of some kind. What else was under there?

"I found him," Brian said into the handset. "Yeah. He looks all right. Couple scrapes, maybe. Looks like he fell or something. He's down by the gate. I think he's trying to leave."

"I'm not leaving. I'm not going anywhere. And who are you talking to?" Arman demanded. "Why are you following me?"

Brian put the walkie-talkie away. "I'm following you, idiot, because it seems there are some questions that you need to answer."

"Well, what if I was leaving? How would that be any of your business?"

"It'd be my business because I'd have to stop you."

"With a gun?"

"You think I need a *gun* to stop you? Yeah, okay. Maybe you are delusional, kid. Let's go." He took a step toward the now-open gate.

"Why should I listen to you?" Arman called after him.

Brian didn't look back. "What choice do you have?"

Arman had no answer for that, and so he was marched back to his own cabin, where the lights were on. Kira and Dale were standing around worriedly, along with Mari, the dark-haired woman, and Dr. Gary. It was basically a shitshow of every single person he didn't want to see at the moment.

"What are you doing?" he asked them.

"Where were you?" Kira's eyes were wide. "We couldn't find you."

"Why do you care where I was?" He looked around the room. "Why do any of you care? It's the middle of the night."

"Sit down," Dr. Gary said.

"What?"

"I said sit down." His tone was firm. "We need to talk to you."

Arman sat on his cot. Held his stomach.

Mari sat beside him. The cot springs squeaked and sank beneath her weight. "Arman, Beau didn't show up in San Francisco today."

He stared at her. "What?"

"The person he was supposed to be meeting with called us. He hasn't shown up. And no one can reach him on his phone."

Arman glanced up. Everyone was looking at him.

"Did you hear what I said?" Mari asked.

"I heard you. And I already told you what happened. So it's not surprising that he didn't show up. He's not going to. I wish that weren't the case. I really do. But it is."

Mari winced. "If something happened, you can talk to us about it. That's all you need to do. Just be honest."

"I am being honest! I swear."

"I warned Beau about this," muttered the dark-haired woman. "Bringing kids here for no reason. They don't know what they're doing. They never want to listen."

"He had to know we couldn't use them all," Dr. Gary said. "I mean, look at them. It's not like they're—"

"Enough!" Mari glared at them both. Then she turned back to Arman, her expression softening. "Please, dear. You know I care about you. You know you can talk to me."

Arman's chest felt like an overfilled balloon. "But I told you what I know. I told you everything that happened!"

Dr. Gary huffed. "That stuff about the van disappearing? Come on."

"But it's *true*. I was just down by the road right now. There are fresh burn marks from the tires. I made those! When I was driving!"

"Burn marks?"

"Yes! I can show you!"

"Why would I care about burn marks?"

"The kid was leaving," Brian said. "He'd climbed the gate."

"I wasn't leaving!"

"Yes, you were."

"Fuck you!" he snarled.

"Arman!" Mari snapped, something he'd never seen her do.

"I'm sorry," he said quickly. "I didn't mean it."

But of course he did.

The adults left soon after, but not before imposing the dark promise of *further discussion* and a reminder that no one was to leave the compound without permission. Arman understood full well that "no one" meant him. He mumbled agreement but could tell the trainers still weren't happy with him. That was a feeling he hated, but he didn't know *how* to make them happy. Telling the truth wasn't the answer. They wanted a truth he knew was a lie. that he knew where Beau was. That something had happened between them that meant Arman would be foolish enough to come back to the compound and make up some outlandish story about suicide and head wounds and vanishing vans.

Or desperate enough.

Arman lay on his cot and rolled away from his roommates. His head hurt more than ever.

Kira crouched beside him.

"Arman," she whispered. "Why didn't you tell us what happened? You talked to both Dale and me, and you didn't tell us *anything*."

"So?"

"So . . . don't you see how it looks?"

"No, Kira. Why don't you tell me how it looks?"

"It looks bad," she said. "It looks really bad."

He rolled back over to face her. "Well, what am I supposed to do? Do you think I *like* this? First I'm told I'm crazy. That I hit my head and made everything up. Then I'm told that I . . . I don't even know!"

"Well, I don't *know* what you think. Because you don't say anything about yourself. *Ever.* But I do know that you need to come clean about whatever it is you did—"

Arman sat up. "I didn't do anything! Stop saying that!"

"Don't yell at her," Dale growled from across the cabin.

"I'm not yelling! She's pissing me off!"

Kira got to her feet. Stared down at Arman with her arms crossed. "I knew you shouldn't have come here. I didn't want you to. I even told Dale what you were like back home."

"Oh yeah? What am I like?"

"You're always ruining shit because you don't know how to be normal! It's annoying. Some of us want to be here, you know. If you don't, then go. But don't make us all miserable just because you are."

It felt like a rash had broken out all over his body. "You don't know the kind of things that go on around here, Kira. I mean it. You don't. Not everyone's like Beau. Some of these people, they just want your money."

She scoffed. "So you're the expert? You know better than me, when I'm the one who's actually been following this program while you've been running around doing God knows what and taking pain pills?"

He flared. "A doctor gave me those pills!"

"I bet."

"You don't know what you're talking about."

Kira lifted her chin. "I know you didn't pay to be here, not like the rest of us. So maybe *you* don't get to lecture me."

"He didn't pay?" Dale asked.

"No, he didn't." Kira turned around. "That woman trainer told me she looked at the books and he was the only one who hadn't paid. She wanted to know if I knew why, so I told her he must've lied his way in here somehow. That's he's no better than his felon father."

"Don't say that!" That was it. Arman was on his feet, ready to charge.

Dale leapt across the cabin. Grabbed on to him by the shirt collar. "What the hell do you think you're doing?"

"Nothing!"

"You're acting crazy, you know that? Like really crazy."

Arman squirmed. "I'm not like my dad! She needs to take that back!"

"I'm not taking anything back," Kira said.

"Look," Dale told him. "I don't care about your dad. I don't care about any of this. You just need to calm down."

Arman wrenched himself free from Dale's grip. Sat back on his cot with his heart pounding. "I am calm."

"Good."

"I'm going to sleep now."

Dale nodded. "That's good, too, Arman. You do that."

28

WHEN ARMAN OPENED HIS EYES the next morning, the first thing on his mind was the cook. And he wasn't thinking about whether he'd knocked her up or contracted herpes or if he'd be lucky enough to get another shot at trying to do both. No, he was thinking about the fact that he hadn't told her about Beau. That he hadn't told her anything. Now that other people knew Beau was missing, it meant she might find out, too. If Arman didn't tell her what he knew first, there was no predicting what she might make of it.

Or of *him*.

The coil of dread squeezing his rib cage got Arman to haul ass out of bed and make his way down to the dining hall in a hurry. He managed to leave before Dale and Kira were even awake, for which he was grateful. He was in no mood to continue their argument from the night before.

Walking through the meadow beneath a foggy sky, Arman went over what he might say to the cook and how he might say it. He just needed to sneak a quick moment of privacy with her, before all hell broke loose. Before everyone started looking at him the way Kira and the trainers had looked at him last night—like he was *guilty*.

Like he'd done something bad.

Breakfast was served outside. Food and drink were laid out on tables located at the main dining hall entrance. While this arrangement was preferable to sitting with strangers, it also kept Arman from slinking into the kitchen from the garden. With everyone standing around, he'd be in plain view.

So much for privacy.

He took two sweet rolls and a cup of juice and lingered on the edge of the crowd. He ate quickly and swallowed his Paxil and Adderall when no one was looking. Scanning the group with what he hoped was discretion, Arman strained to spot the river-pebble-eye guy. But he didn't. He was about to start walking through the crowd, to search more, when he was stopped by the old man he'd sat with at dinner the night before.

"Oh, hey," he said, because the old man had grabbed his arm, sloshing his juice onto the ground. The guy was stronger than he looked.

"I *know* you," the man said.

Arman smiled. "Yes, you do. We talked last night."

"We did?"

"We talked about love-shyness. You told me not to throw up around girls."

The man made a face. All that wrinkled skin. "That's not it. I recognize you from back home."

"Back home in Oakland?"

"That's right."

"Well, I'm not from Oakland."

"You got arrested recently, didn't you? That's where I know you from. You were in jail."

"Wait, what?" Arman stared at him. "In jail? No, I wasn't. I've never been *arrested*."

The old man made a clucking sound. "Oh, I never forget a face, son. You were charged with . . . oh, now, let's see. What was it again?"

"*Nothing*. I wasn't charged with anything because it wasn't *me*. I'm only seventeen. And I've never done anything wrong." This was a lie, of course, but no one needed to know that but him.

"A pyramid scheme!" The old man pointed right at Arman with glee, pleased to have solved the mystery. At the victorious sound of his voice, people around them turned to look. "That was it, wasn't it? You were running it out of Emeryville. Something to do with self-hypnosis tapes, am I right? Or was it something else? Drugs charges, maybe?"

"No." Arman yanked his arm free. Took a flustered step backward. People were still staring. They weren't looking away. "I never did anything like that. I swear."

"You sure?"

"I'm sure," Arman insisted, although his body was starting to do its sweating thing. He lowered his voice to a hiss. "That wasn't me. You're talking about my *father*."

"Your father?"

"Yeah."

There was no flicker of recognition in the old man's rheumy eyes. He simply shrugged. Wandered off.

Left alone, Arman glanced around like a caged beast. It was like being up on the mountain again, standing in a circle of so many staring eyes. All that watching. Judging. Holding him under scrutiny he couldn't begin to read.

Are they looking at me like that because of my dad?

Or do they know about Beau?

———

A bell rang, a soft chiming. The signal to head into the meeting hall, apparently. The group watching Arman turned and walked away without further incident. No one said a word.

He trailed after them but felt sour. Bitter, really. Arman's Before Life wasn't meant to have followed him here. It was the last thing he wanted to deal with. Back at school he'd lived in constant fear that people would find out what kind of person his dad was. A junkie. A deadbeat. A college burnout who, after being handed every advantage in life, couldn't keep a job or stay sober and instead used his earnest face and sweet voice to hustle drugs and smooth-talk old ladies and college students into giving him money they couldn't afford in exchange for promises that had no hope of coming true. Lying was his father's one true gift, it turned out, elevated by the art of delusion. How could he live with himself otherwise?

Inside the dome, everyone sat cross-legged on the floor. Arman braced himself for some sort of meditation or guided exercise like they'd been asked to do at Vespers the night before. Instead they were broken into smaller groups and put to work. Real physical labor. Dr. Gary mumbled something about the importance of "maintaining a standard of health in every dimension of vitality," but Arman was skeptical. Getting people to chop firewood and pick weeds in the garden seemed more like a ploy to get basic chores done than a genuine step toward self-actualization.

Then again, some of the groups were given more rigorous assignments: shoring up the fence perimeter on the eastern side of the property, cleaning the cannon, and taking inventory of all the canned goods and seeds that were in underground storage. Arman's own group, which unfortunately included Dale, got the worst job of all: They were directed to dig out four six-foot deep cylindrical holes at the top of the sun-scorched hill overlooking the gravel drive so that the concrete footings for a "Surveillance and Communications Tower" could be poured.

So maybe this was about more than basic chores.

As he pushed a wheelbarrow filled with work gloves and shovels from the toolshed, Arman spotted Mari standing on the walkway outside the dome. She hadn't been in there when the work assignments were handed out, which was strange. At the moment, she looked lost. Or confused. Something. Either way, he made sure to duck his head as he passed by her. The last thing he wanted was to make eye contact.

At the worksite, Arman did as he was told. Pounding the clay dirt with a pickax couldn't be good for his concussion, but he didn't complain. No one around him seemed to know anything about Beau, and he intended to keep it that way. Arman swung helplessly at the hard-packed earth, which refused to make a dent under his efforts.

Dale, as usual, couldn't keep his mouth shut.

"What did you say we're doing this for?" he growled after they'd been working for almost an hour. He leaned on his shovel with gloved hands, and his face, streaked with sweat and dirt, wore an unmistakable fuck-this-shit expression.

The leader of the group gave him a flat look. "I told you. We're building a structure. These holes are going to be for the support posts, and Gary wants you to dig them. So go on and dig already."

"Yeah, but you called it a 'Surveillance Tower' before."

"Surveillance and Communication."

"So who's being surveilled?"

"Who says it's a who?"

"What?"

"That's exactly right. Maybe it's a what. Not a who."

"Jesus. Well, then *what's* being watched?"

The man shrugged. "Don't know. Maybe fires."

"*Fires?* Are you kidding me?"

"That's right."

Dale looked around. "Anyone else buying this shit?"

No one said anything.

Dale shook his head in disgust.

Went back to digging.

29

ARMAN MANAGED TO GET AWAY as the sun broke through the clouds. He begged off by saying he had to use the restroom.

The group leader appeared unimpressed. "You can't find a tree, kid?"

"Nope." Arman scampered off, heading up the meadow trail toward the circle of cabins and the A-framed bathroom. He hid in one of the stalls for a while, in part because he really did have to go, but also so nobody could accuse him of lying about his whereabouts. The appearance of honesty, his dad always told him, was far more important than the truth.

There were two places the cook could be. Seeing as the kitchen was the more difficult location to access, Arman visited her cabin first. He went up the same way he had last night—by cutting through the woods and hiking around the research building. But Arman froze as he passed beneath the building's stone pilings.

He heard voices.

They were coming from outside the building's front entrance. Flattening his back against the cement wall so that he stayed in shadows, Arman peeked around the corner. He strained to see who it was or hear what they were saying, but they were too far away. The voices faded as the group walked inside, leaving only the faint clodding of the human herd. Arman thought he caught a flash of long braids as they left, lit by the late-morning sun.

Then they were gone.

Arman didn't have to knock on the cook's window to find her. She was already outside, sitting by herself on the cabin's rickety front porch, reading a book. Arman's breath caught at the sight. The essence of summer—she sat beneath a wall of climbing ivy, and her bare legs stuck straight out, twisting in the milky sunshine as she stared down at the book's pages, lost in a world only she could know.

She looked up then, and she saw him. Only she wasn't scared this time. She didn't jump or yell or back away. Instead their eyes met and her lips did that twitching thing. Not a smile, exactly. But not *not* one, either.

Oh God.

"No one saw me come up here," he said thickly.

"Good." She set her book aside.

Arman shuffled closer to where she sat but remained standing. There was so much he needed to say, but he was having trouble thinking. It was overwhelming. Her presence. Her closeness. Her everything.

He stared at her thighs. That felt safest.

"You left last night," she said.

"I know."

"Why?"

Arman shrugged. He felt awkward all of a sudden and sort of horrible about it. Was there a right answer to her question? If there was, it's not like he would ever say it. Besides, that wasn't what he'd come to talk about.

"How's your head?" she asked.

"Better, I guess."

"I'm worried about Beau."

This was a startling statement. Arman stared at her. "Why?"

"He hasn't gotten in touch since he left yesterday. And he usually does." The cook reached up, took Arman by the hand, and pulled him down next to her. "I tried asking those assholes about it. But they wouldn't tell me anything."

"What assholes?"

"You know, the trainers. I've decided to stop being scared of them, by the way. They can't tell me what to do. I know Beau won't let them get rid of me, so I don't care if they like me." She raised her chin. "Which they don't."

"Oh," Arman said weakly. "Well, that's kind of what I wanted to talk to you about. I didn't want you to hear it from anyone else. Especially them."

She cocked her head. "Hear what?"

"That Beau's missing."

"Huh?"

"Mari said he didn't get where he was going yesterday. I guess she heard from the person he was supposed to meet in San Francisco. And see, there was this thing that happened yesterday, when I left here. I don't totally understand it, and I thought maybe it was because I hit my head. That's what Gary said. That's why I didn't tell you."

She held his hand tighter. "Tell me what, Arman?"

"That I saw him yesterday. After I left."

"You saw Beau?"

Arman nodded. "I ran into him while I was walking down to the highway. He was going to give me a ride. But when I got in the van to go with him, he'd cut himself. With a knife. Really bad. There was blood . . . everywhere. I thought he was dead. I really did, and I drove up here with him, but by the time I found help, the van was gone."

"What do you mean gone?"

"I mean, it was just *gone*. Vanished. With Beau in it. There was no trace it'd ever been here in the first place. It didn't make sense. It still doesn't. And my head was bleeding, see? I didn't know how I'd hurt it, so everyone told me I was just confused. That the things I remembered couldn't be true and that I didn't really know what had happened."

The cook blinked. Then took a deep breath. "Who told you this?"

"Them! The trainers. Gary and Mari and that woman."

"*They* told you you were confused?"

"Yes."

"And they're the ones who said Beau didn't get where he was supposed to go?"

Arman nodded.

The cook said nothing. She sat there in silence, with her cheeks flushed and her jaw clenched. She sat that way for so long that Arman started to get worried.

"Are you okay?" he asked.

"No." She jerked her head toward him. Her eyes were hot and her cheeks wet. "I'm not okay. Not at all. I'm going to *fucking* kill them."

"Wait, what?" Arman said. "No, you can't do that. Why would you do that?"

"What do you mean why? You're telling me they murdered Beau!" Her voice choked.

"But I didn't say anything about *murder*. He killed himself. He cut his own wrists!"

The cook gave him a how-stupid-are-you look. "You think Beau just happened to cut his wrists right before he was going to give you a ride? And that even though nobody knew he was going to do this, someone was waiting to hide him and the van the moment you got back here?"

Arman was flustered. "No. I—I don't know. I hadn't thought about it."

"Well, I am thinking about it. That's the only thing that makes sense." Her nostrils flared. "Someone's coming."

Arman glanced up. Sure enough, there was a figure running toward them. Well, sort of running. Whoever it was moved with a weird loping gait, like their shoes didn't fit right or they'd forgotten the basics of human locomotion. It was *Dale*, Arman realized, as the person drew closer. What was he doing here? Clearly not an athlete, he pulled up in front of Arman and the cook, then doubled over, grabbing his chest and gasping for air.

"Come on." He wheezed and gestured to Arman. "You . . . need . . . to . . . come . . . with . . . me."

"You need to stop smoking."

"Very . . . funny." Dale managed to stand upright as he gestured again. "But I'm serious."

"You're never serious."

"That's not true. And this is important. So come on, already."

"How'd you find me?" Arman asked. "I didn't tell you where I was going."

Dale's gaze drifted to the cook. "Wasn't all that hard."

Arman turned to look at her. He hated to see the pain on her face. It made him feel guilty, even though he'd done nothing wrong. "I'm sorry," he told her. "I guess I have to go. But there's more we need to talk about. A lot more. He could be fine. Really."

Tears still welled in her eyes. "You think?"

"I don't *know*. I mean, that's just it. A lot of what I remember doesn't make sense. So please. Just don't do or say anything. Not yet. Not until I know more."

She bit her lip. Nodded. "You better find me later. Please, Arman."

"I will. I promise." Arman squeezed her hand, then got up to go with

Dale. They began jogging back down toward the main path.

"You okay?" Dale asked.

"I'm fine."

"You sure?"

"I just said I was."

"I'm not pissed at you, you know. I mean, about last night."

"Glad to hear it."

"Are *you* pissed at me?"

"No," Arman said. "I'm not. That's not what I'm thinking about at all, actually."

"Good."

"Seriously, though. How'd you know I was with her?"

Dale grinned. "Shit, man. Wasn't hard. That chick's the only girl under forty around here and you don't strike me as the cougar type."

"Oh." Arman jogged faster. He wasn't sure what surprised him more: that Dale guessed he was with a girl or the fact that he was right. "Where did you say we're going?"

"I didn't say. But I was told to come get you. I think you're going to want to see this."

"See what?"

"They found Beau's van."

THE YET UNKNOWN.

During the time they're in the cell together, two very different ships passing in the night, you can easily imagine that the hopeless man keeps talking and talking. That he doesn't know how to stop because he doesn't understand how others might see him. Or judge him.

Or else he doesn't care.

You wonder how it can be that he has no questions of his own. That he doesn't pause and ask the wise man sitting across from him "who are you?" and "why are you listening to me?"

But you also know he'd never do that. It's not that he couldn't, it's that he has no interest in a man in whom he sees no advantage. No way to exploit. Besides, he's always believed the world's against him, a flaw that's ensured he's never tried to make the world a better place. A flaw that absolves him of guilt. But he's not without skill, of course. In fact, with his sweet face and even sweeter voice, he's very convincing.

These are all the reasons the wise man listens so closely.

I could've easily been this man, the wise man thinks. If I'd been more bitter. If I'd been left alone in my bitterness during my darkest times. But he wasn't left alone. When he was young and reckless and found himself in trouble, there was a young public defender named Virgil, who had different skin and a different upbringing, but who nonetheless saw his pain and potential and helped him thrive. He won't ever forget that gift. It's what taught him that there were two kinds of fathers in this world. The ones you can't help.

And the ones you'd die for.

The wise man knows it's too late for his cellmate. For his redemption. And reform. Those are roads he won't travel. Those are regrets he won't face. But when he hears that the talking man has a child—a boy—he's interested again.

"My own son doesn't like me," the talking man says. "He used to, you know. When he was younger. Those were the days. Kid's the spitting image of me, and he looked out for me back then. Did anything I wanted without me even asking. One time I got pulled over for speeding and I was holding, you know? Would've been bad if the car'd been searched. Real bad. But you know what my kid tells the cop when he comes to the window? Just all on his own?"

"What?" the wise man asks.

"Without missing a damn beat, kid pipes up that he's diabetic. That he's on the verge of a seizure, and I'm taking him to get his insulin. Of all things. Then he bats those big brown eyes of his like a fucking angel. Cop let us go right then and there."

"Ah."

"He's not diabetic, of course. Kid was goddamn perfect back then. Don't even know where he came up with that," the man says proudly, before his voice turns dark. "He's not like that anymore, though. Now he's weak. Doesn't care what I say. Doesn't want my help. It's his mother's fault. He even cut himself to get away from me. So that he wouldn't have to see me. You believe that shit?"

The wise man says nothing in response. He's wise for a reason, after all. But in his mind, he's thinking: Smart boy. That's a very smart boy.

Even if he doesn't know it yet.

30

THEY LEFT DALE BEHIND AT the compound, an act Arman was sure he'd appreciate, seeing as the van he was currently riding in was twisting high into the mountains on the most narrow of two-lane roads. Heights were bountiful. As was tension. Arman, on the other hand, longed for Dale's company. Or the company of *someone* he trusted. Someone who didn't hate him or think he was awful. Then he wouldn't feel so anxious.

Or vulnerable.

Sitting squeezed in the back between Mari and Dr. Gary, Arman did his best to avoid conversation. Hell, he was practically avoiding breathing, hoping to be forgotten the way he'd been forgotten in all those classrooms back at school. The longer the drive went on, the more the cook's accusations swirled through his brain. She'd accused these very people of *murder*. Actual murder. And what if they *weren't* going to see a van that Brian claimed to have discovered? What if they were taking him somewhere else?

Alone.

Arman focused on keeping his legs from shaking. His hands, too. If he didn't return from this ride, no one would miss him. There was no one *to* miss him. Dale himself said he didn't worry about things and Kira was mad at him. And it wasn't like the cops would be looking for him, seeing as his last act out in civilization involved stealing from his stepdad, who wasn't likely to file a police report. The cook might notice his absence, sure, but she wouldn't feel any sort of loss. How could she? They'd met all of two days ago. Arman couldn't even get her to tell him her name, and so far her interest in *him* hadn't extended past the things she could get him to do with his hands and his mouth and his dick. It wasn't like she'd taken a deep interest in his stunning intellect or charming wit.

Brian kept driving. Higher and higher. Supposedly, he was taking them to a spot he'd found that skimmed the border of the vast Los Padres National Forest. A very isolated spot, it seemed, far from the compound in a gloomy place where the hills were steeper, the trees denser, and everything felt more foreboding.

More dangerous.

Staring out the van window, at so much loneliness, Arman's shaking grew worse.

"It's up here." Brian finally pulled into a turnout on a crumbling section of road. The four of them stepped into the spotty sunshine, thick rays that dripped through the branches of the towering redwood trees to scald their skin and make them sweat. The air smelled faintly of smoke. Brian gestured toward the roadside edge, urging them to follow.

Arman walked forward but felt numb. Was this it then? Was this the end? He considered the ways it might happen. A gunshot to the back of his head, perhaps. Or a sharp push. It didn't matter. His brain spun with images of that hockey goalie again. The one who'd gotten his throat cut on the ice. He'd survived that horror only to try to kill himself years later, and for all Arman's thoughts on suicide, maybe fate had its own plans, free will be damned. Maybe that's all life was meant to be: a race to the end and nothing more.

But gazing over the cliff's edge, straight down into the depths of a remote craggy canyon, Arman saw what he least expected to. Not the life-flashing slideshow of his own demise, rather, he spotted a *van*. An actual white passenger van. What was left of one, anyway. Far below, amid slick rock and deep shadows, in a spot unreachable by foot, the vehicle lay flipped onto its roof, flattened and charred.

Dr. Gary and Mari gathered on either side of Arman to look. They wore twin expressions of shock, but Arman let out a long exhalation of relief. Death, it seemed, was not imminent.

Then why was he still shaking?

"How'd you find it?" Dr. Gary asked, and his voice was hushed. Solemn.

Brian cleared his throat. "You told me to look for anything unusual, so I stopped at every turnout on the cliff side of the road. I was looking for places where someone could push a vehicle over the edge and not have anyone notice."

"Could it have been an accident?"

"Maybe. I don't know what it was. But there aren't any skid marks. And why would Beau have been driving *up* the mountain if he was heading toward San Francisco? It doesn't make sense."

"So you're sure it's Beau's? Do you really think he's down there?"

"I'm not sure of *anything*. All I know is this kid said a van was missing. And now this."

This kid. Arman wrapped his arms around himself. The drumbeat pulse of pain had returned to his head. He knew what they were thinking about him and he knew it wasn't true, but even he was struggling to come up with an alternative hypothesis. At least one anyone might begin to believe.

I didn't do it, he wanted to say, but denying something made people see you as guilty, didn't it? That's what they'd said about Nixon and his "I am not a crook" line. He'd said that on national television, and no one believed him.

Then again, Arman reminded himself with a shudder, Nixon *was* a crook.

They drove back to the compound in silence. Arman didn't look out the window this time. He didn't look anywhere. He just stared at his lap and the jittery shadows cast there, that strange interplay of dark and light.

The dark-haired woman sprinted toward them the moment they pulled into the parking lot.

"What happened?" she asked, grabbing on to the open window with both hands. "What'd you find?"

Dr. Gary stepped out of the van first. He put a hand on her shoulder as he explained what they'd found. Her face went pale. Her hand went to her mouth.

"What are we going to *do*?" she breathed.

Dr. Gary looked her in the eye. "We need to stay calm. There are contingencies in place for everything. You know what the next steps are, right?"

The woman nodded.

"Good. Then we need to get started. The sooner, the better. Change is up to us. Just us. It always has been."

"But are you sure?" she asked. "Are you really sure?"

"Of course I'm sure," he told her. "It's what Beau would want. For his work to go on. To evolve without him."

The woman nodded again, but her shoulders were slumped. Her normal haughtiness gone.

"Yeah, but aren't you going to . . . ," Arman started, but then let his question trail off. He was going to say *call the cops*. But like his stepfather, he got the feeling calling the cops was the last thing anyone here was planning on doing.

Especially now.

"Arman," Mari said, and while she didn't walk over and squeeze his arm, he still imagined he could read kindness in her eyes. A stern sort of kindness—tough love or whatever—and maybe this was what it was like to have an adult in his life who cared enough to be disappointed when he screwed up. "I think you'd better go wait in your cabin. We'll come get you if we need you."

Arman nodded, but swallowed hard. "Maybe I should just, you know, get my things and go."

"No way," she said, and whatever he'd mistaken for kindness was gone now. Vanished in an instant, if it'd ever been there in the first place. "No goddamn way. You're not going anywhere until we tell you to."

31

I'M ALIVE. I'M STILL ALIVE.

But why?

Arman paced the cabin floor. He had no idea how long he'd been in here, but the sun was fading and his mind was racing. He couldn't figure out what was going on. Or why. Because if the cook was right about Beau being murdered, that meant Arman was a witness, albeit a confused one. So why *wouldn't* the trainers want to get rid of him?

But they hadn't.

The only way Arman could make sense of this fact was that not all three of the people who'd been in the van with him were in on it. That whoever the guilty party was intended to frame Arman. Play dumb and let the others believe *he* did something to Beau. Then they were probably planning to deal with Arman later. On their own.

And no one would care.

Fuck.

It wasn't like Arman didn't know who the killer was. Only one person who'd been in that van was currently enacting their "contingency plan" now that Beau was gone. Only one person who had the arrogance to state that his spiritual faith pointed inward—that he was literally *his own god*. Gary must have an accomplice, though. Someone other than the dark-haired woman. Someone who'd moved the van when Arman arrived at the compound. Not Brian, obviously— he was the one who'd grabbed Arman in the domed meeting hall— but maybe another one of the guards. Or someone else completely. Maybe someone who—

Hold up, hold up, hold up. Wait a minute. Just stop. Stop all of this.

A cloud of darkness rolled over Arman, halting him in his tracks and filling him with sudden doubt. This whole thing, everything he was thinking, it was all completely *insane*. Wasn't it? That's what it felt like, because the picture starting to form in Arman's mind looked a hell of a lot like one of those conspiracy theories his narcissist father liked to concoct in order to maintain his belief that everything revolved around *him*. Those theories were about as real as his father's jazz club in Belize. But the thing was, Arman *knew* nothing revolved around him. He knew he wasn't important. Yet here he still was, his mind bursting with wild thoughts of murder and accomplices and alibis. But maybe it was like the old man had explained at dinner yesterday—in fearing irrelevancy, Arman's mind made this whole thing up.

How pathetic would that be?

Arman collapsed on his cot. His chest was heavy and his will despairing. He reached to pull his Paxil out of his bag and poured the pills onto his bed. He counted them, *tick, tick, tick.* There were eighteen total.

Then he dug around for the rest of his medication: There was the Adderall and the Dexilant and those powerful painkillers he'd been given for his head. He dumped all of them out. Every last one. Counted again. Thirty-two total.

Arman stared at the pills. They stared right back at him.

Like sixteen pairs of wicked eyes.

Oh God, he thought.

Life was about autonomy and joy, wasn't it? Competence and connectedness. Both Beau and the cook had told him that. And Arman believed them. But believing meant that from where he stood, whether the nightmare that had trapped him existed in the external world or merely inside his own mind, didn't much matter. What mattered—the only thing—was the fact that, either way, he was completely screwed.

Arman had just placed the first pill in his mouth when the cabin door banged open, making him jump. He spit out the pill, one of the Paxils. It spun across the floor.

"Goddamn it!" Kira stormed in like a wildfire, bellowing at the top of her lungs. As she crossed the room, she snatched an empty water glass from the table. Threw it against the wall as hard as she could. Glass shattered everywhere.

"Jesus." Dale trailed behind her, looking shell-shocked. "Can you not do that?"

Arman stared at the scene with wide eyes. He'd never seen Kira so mad. Not even last night.

"What's wrong?" he asked.

"Everything!" she snapped. "Fucking everything's wrong!"

"Oh." A stone was sweating in Arman's stomach. He went to dig at his arm. Forgetting what was going on and what they'd caught him in the middle of doing, more than anything, he had an awful fear of getting yelled at.

The worst.

Dale glanced over at him. "You look like you're going to puke, dude."

That's what it felt like. Arman dug harder. "Did I do something? I'm sorry about last night. I am. I'm really, really sorry."

Kira scowled. "Don't be sorry. *I'm* the one who's sorry. I should be thanking you, you know."

"Me? For what?"

"For telling me the truth! You said these people were assholes. That they just wanted my money. Well, you were right."

"I was?"

"Yes," she said. "And now they're going to wish they'd never heard of me."

"What happened?"

Kira ground her shoe into a piece of broken glass. "I was invited to a 'special' meeting this morning is what happened. While you guys were building latrines or whatever, they took a bunch of us into this weird building in the woods, to sit in some sort of upstairs lounge. First, we did some bonding exercise, which was fine. But then the guy in charge started talking about something called 'Containment,' which means closing the compound and just living here on our own. Without being able to leave! He said we'd been chosen to be a part of this new vision and that we all had special gifts that could help advance the human mind. It wasn't hard to figure out he meant money. Then he had us each use the phone to call our family and ask them to donate their own 'gifts' to support our growth."

"Seriously?"

"I told him I was here because I didn't want to depend on my dad. That that was *my* way of evolving. But rather than supporting me, he told me how disappointed he was and how maybe I wasn't ready for true change. I guess shame's good when it serves his needs, right? Well, then I asked him what about all the other people here? And he said not everyone was a 'good fit' for the program. That some would be 'reabsorbed.' Then I realized he meant Dale. And you."

"'Reabsorbed?'" Arman echoed.

She nodded, and right then, Dale, who'd been rummaging around under his cot, crawled back out with a rolled joint in his hand. He stuck it in his mouth and lit up. Passed it to Kira, who took it gratefully.

"Screw them," she said, shutting her eyes and inhaling as hard as she could. "Let's be the stupid kids they think we are for once. Even if we don't know what we're doing, we're still smarter than the rest of them."

"A-fucking-men," said Dale.

Kira let the joint dangle from her lips. "Just wait till I tell my dad about this. He's gonna shit bricks."

"Wait. So you *are* going to talk to him?" Arman asked.

"Not to get money. I'm going to get him to sue the hell out of this place. It's nothing but a scam."

"Oh."

"Hey, what's all this?" Dale pointed at the pills spilled out on Arman's cot.

"It's nothing," he said.

"This stuff any good?" Dale picked up the empty bottle of Dexilant.

"It's my *heartburn* medicine."

Dale shrugged. Put it down. Fingered the Adderall bottle.

Kira stared at the pills, too. But she frowned. "Arman . . ."

"I don't want to talk about it," he said. "And stop touching my shit already."

Dale scrambled to his feet. "Guess Kira's not the only one in a pissy mood."

"I guess not."

"Well, why the hell's that?"

"I already said I don't want to talk about it!"

"Fine. Jesus."

"Here." Kira tapped Arman on the shoulder. Held out the lit joint as an offering. "I think you need this. Maybe more than I do."

Arman had never smoked before. He hesitated before taking it.

But only for a moment.

32

"SO, YOU GOING TO TELL us what happened with that van or what?" Kira asked. They were all sitting on the floor in the middle of the cabin, and Dale had his head in her lap.

Arman passed the joint to him and released the smoke from his lungs with a gasp. He'd been holding it for as long as he could, which was what they'd told him to do. It felt sharp inside of him, crackling and hot, like a burning cactus had taken up residence inside his chest.

"Nothing happened," he said. "Nothing good."

"But you went to go see it, right? That's what Dale said. Was it really Beau's?"

Arman shook his head. "I shouldn't— I don't think I'm supposed to talk about it."

"Suit yourself," Kira said with a shrug.

But Dale sat up then, his eyes squinting as smoke streamed into his face. "What do you mean *suit yourself*? He should definitely talk to us about what's going on. He absolutely should."

"Well, he won't," Kira told him.

"How do you know?"

"Because when it comes to secrets, Arman's a master at holding them."

"Why do you say that?" Dale asked, and Arman stared at her. He was wondering the same thing.

Kira plucked the joint from Dale's mouth. Sucked on it. "Because when we were in fourth grade, Arman and I were in the same class. Ms. Vasquez. She had this pet guinea pig. Her name was Bella, and we all took turns feeding her and cleaning her cage. Well, I guess Bella must've died the week Arman was taking care of her. I don't know how. I think she was old." She glanced at Arman, but he said nothing. His mouth was too dry and his head felt heavy, like it was on the verge of falling into some unseen abyss. Plus he wanted to hear what Kira had to say. He knew where the story was going. He'd just never known if anyone had understood.

"Anyway," she said. "Instead of telling us what happened, he let us all believe Bella had escaped. We left food out for her and set up cameras at night so we could see where she was. But we found nothing, obviously."

"So where was she?" Dale asked.

"Arman had hidden her in his desk, under some of his books. Ms. Vasquez finally figured it out when Bella started to stink."

Dale blew smoke through his nostrils, then burst out laughing. "Oh, shit. Why'd you do that, man?"

Arman shrugged.

"He did it because he was scared," Kira said. "He was too scared to do anything. So he did nothing."

She did understand. Arman realized, dropping his heavy head back to stare at the ceiling. *She really did.* Closing his eyes, he coasted as best he could—attempting to ward off the darkness by steering his mind clear of the future while not wallowing in the past. And all the while, he used his index finger to carve into the skin around his collarbone.

Deep.

Deep.

Deeper.

Then Arman's eyes flew open and he sat straight up. Struck by sudden inspiration. "Look," he said, surprising himself more than anyone else in the room. "How about this? I'll tell you guys what happened with the van. I'll tell you everything. Not about Bella, but about Beau and the truth of what's been going on around here. Okay? I'll tell you because I really need your help."

By the time he was done explaining, Dale and Kira were both staring at him in disbelief.

"You think you walked in on Beau's murder?" Kira worked her jaw, as if her mouth needed to process the words along with her brain. "I mean, a scam is one thing, but this is sort of , . . I don't know, Arman. It's a *lot*. It's kind of a leap."

"But I'm not the only one who thinks so! The cook, she believes it, too. She says the trainers have been trying to get rid of Beau for a while now."

"But you said you don't think it's all of the trainers? Just this one?"

He nodded. "The guy you had the meeting with. Who told you to call your dad and get money."

"And who's this cook?" Kira asked.

Dale grinned. "That's Arman's girlfriend."

"Arman has a *girlfriend*?"

"She's not my girlfriend," Arman said. "But she could get hurt. Someone could hurt her."

"What do you want to do?" Dale asked.

"I want to get her away from here. And I want to go to the cops. But first I need proof of what happened to Beau. That *I* didn't do it."

"Do you have proof?"

"No. But I think I know where to look."

"What about us?" Kira asked. "They're going to be closing this place off soon."

"Just act normal. Follow the program. Pretend you don't know anything about me. And I'll be getting help. It won't take long. If the cops aren't here by breakfast tomorrow, that means something happened to me. Then you guys should go. Kira, you should call your dad. Raise as much hell as you can."

She snorted. "Oh, I will absolutely do that."

"Thank you." Arman felt jittery again. Restless. Just talking about the situation, his fears, made him want to move, get moving, do *something*. He had a plan, after all, a real plan.

For once.

33

KIRA LEFT FIRST. THE SKY had turned dark, and it was her job to find out where everyone was and to report back to Arman before he took off.

While they waited, Arman resumed his pacing. Dale, true to his nature, rolled another joint.

"Have some," he offered. "You need to relax."

Arman shook his head. "I need to be focused. I can't afford to fuck up."

"Focus is overrated."

"Tell that to my mom."

"You're not going to fuck up, dude. You're going to be fine."

"You don't know that!"

Dale lifted an eyebrow. "Christ almighty, kid. Like I said, you need to relax."

Arman's neck went hot. "Look, I get that this is all a joke to you. But this is my life! This is important to me."

"I don't think it's a joke. I think—"

"You think what?"

Dale sighed. "You remember how you helped me climb that rock the other night? When I was scared shitless?"

"Yeah. Sure."

"Well, you didn't make me *not* scared, but what you said let me act. In a way that I wanted to."

Arman returned to pacing. "All right."

"Well, I want to return the favor."

"You are returning the favor. You're helping me. That's enough."

"That's not what I mean."

"Then what do you mean?"

"I mean this." Dale tapped his collarbone, which made Arman reach for his.

"That's nothing," he said, although he cringed to feel the blood there, to know it was seeping through his shirt. "It's stupid."

"I also mean *that*." Dale pointed to the pills still heaped on Arman's bed.

Arman stopped walking. He brushed his hair back, then brushed it back again. "I know what you're thinking, but I'm not going to do anything. I was just frustrated."

"You're sure?"

"I'm absolutely sure. My dad tried to do it once and I hate him for it."

"I'm sorry."

"Don't be. I hate him for a lot of reasons. I'm not like him, you know. At all."

Dale paused. "Okay."

"Okay."

They were both silent for a moment. But it was Arman who spoke next.

"Hey, Dale?"

"Hey, what?"

"Can I ask you something?"

"You can do anything you like."

"What happened to you last night? You said you didn't like this place. You said it was a scam. So why were you so upset?"

"You mean in the meadow?"

"Yeah."

"Oh, I don't know why I was upset exactly. But that thing we did in the tent, sharing secrets we hadn't told anyone. That was *hard*. And not just sharing about myself. But holding someone else's truth. That's heavy shit. Like, really heavy. I wasn't ready for that. You know what I mean?"

Arman nodded. He did know. Of course he did.

Dale took another long drag off the joint. "I guess maybe also something can be a scam but that doesn't mean it has no value."

It wasn't long before Kira returned to the cabin. She looked at Arman.

"You can go now," she said. "They're all in the dining room."

"Everyone's there?" Dale asked. "Even that Gary guy?"

"I think so. Apparently there's some big announcement after dinner. We should get going, too."

Dale put out the joint. Grabbed his sweatshirt and got to his feet.

"Do the guards really have guns?" Arman asked impulsively.

Dale turned around. "That's what I heard."

"Be careful," Kira said. "That Mari lady's looking for you, you know. She's seriously pissed."

"She is?"

"Yup."

"About what?"

"Don't know."

"You sure you want to do this?" Dale asked.

"I have to," Arman said. "It doesn't matter what I want."

"Then we'll see you on the other side, kid." Kira gave a wave as she and Dale slipped out of the cabin into the night.

Then they were gone.

Arman set about gathering up the pills he'd poured out, putting them back in their bottles, then into his bag. Next he grabbed the flashlight from the table, slipping it into the waistband of his pants. It was pitch-black outside. He'd need the light for what he was going to do next.

At last, he left the cabin. Ducked onto the main trail and took off running. His shoes pounded the ground; the night wind was at his back, a howling roar, and perhaps he was fleeing reality as much as he was chasing truth. It broke his heart to know that Mari was mad at him. That she could believe he'd hurt Beau. Arman could only hope that someday she would know of his innocence. Only for that to happen, he had to accomplish his goal tonight.

But what is your goal?

What exactly are you looking for?

Well, he was looking for *proof*, Arman knew. Proof of his innocence and someone else's guilt.

And maybe, he told himself, he was searching for a little bit of relevance, too.

34

WEIGHTED DOWN BY HIS BELONGINGS, Arman eventually slowed to a walk as he made his way through the woods, sweeping beneath the thick coat of darkness, the white trim of stars. Mosquitoes bounced off his cheeks and fluttered through his hair, nipping, sucking as they went. Pieces of the puzzle were coming together for him, and he was headed straight toward the research building. Yesterday, Dr. Gary had said the place wasn't used for anything but storage. But on his first day here, Beau had told him that research at the compound was an ongoing thing. That's what the tuition fees for the classes went toward.

Arman reached the building at last. Standing at the front entrance, he tipped his head back and gazed upward. Unlike the night when he'd walked past here on his way to the cook's, all the rooms on the second floor were dark now. And still.

That was a good thing. A very good thing.

He walked to the front door. Pulled on it.

Locked.

Arman gave a low growl of frustration, but the compound's motto told him what to do. Sidling to his left, he stepped straight into the shrubbery, tamping down branches and snapping twigs as he inched his way along the side of the building. Finally he reached one of the wide metal-rimmed windows that he thought must open into Dr. Gary's office.

But he couldn't be sure.

Hopping up on his toes, Arman tried peering inside. The tempered glass was coated in dust and cobwebs, too thick to see through. He pushed on the window to see if it would give.

It didn't.

More trying was needed. Arman bent down, rooting around on the ground in the dead leaves and dirt until his fingers closed around a grapefruit-sized rock. Sliding his sweatshirt over his head, he wound the whole thing around his hand for protection. Then he gripped the rock and reared back. Punched the window as hard as he could.

The safety glass exploded with a crash. This was followed by a deafening downpour of shards. Like hail falling on asphalt. Heart rattling, Arman twisted his head to look over his shoulder, fully expecting to hear the blare of an alarm or angry voices or the thundering of footsteps running toward him.

But there was nothing.

Still using the sweatshirt, he worked to clear the remaining glass from the frame, dusting it to the ground so that the heavier pieces scattered across his shoes and pinged off rocks. When he was sure he wouldn't get cut, Arman pulled himself up and into the bare window frame, before twisting onto his stomach and sliding to the floor below.

He landed on carpet in complete darkness. Arman fumbled around the room on his hands and knees. His hip bumped a desk, then a filing cabinet before he remembered the flashlight. Yanking it from his waistband, he switched it on. Prayed the light couldn't be seen from the outside.

In the shaky yellow glow Arman saw luck was on his side for once; this *was* Dr. Gary's office. There was no mistaking the site where he'd gotten his stitches. Arman crawled to his feet and shuddered as he moved around the creepy examination chair in the middle of the room.

Reaching the far wall, he began opening cabinet doors, pulling out drawers, poring through the shelves. Looking for anything suspicious. Plans of a coup. Evidence of a conspiracy.

Or foul play.

What he found instead was a shit ton of medical supplies, including what appeared to be a wartime stockpile of medication, which seemed more than a little hinky considering the condescending lecture on mind-body purity Dr. Gary had given him. Apparently the only self-sufficient thing around here was Dr. Gary's ego. Arman spied ample bottles of amphetamines, anxiolytics, sleeping pills, muscle relaxants, even narcotics—really strong stuff. Dangerous, too. His skin prickled, remembering the unnamed painkillers he'd been given with no instruction on how to take them other than "as needed."

Guided by the flashlight, Arman padded over to Dr. Gary's desk, which was piled high with books and papers, a laptop he couldn't get to work, and what appeared to be a vile and rather large collection of musty ceramic mugs with rotting tea bags floating in them. Arman made a face and poked around the mugs carefully. He was loath to spill anything. He also riffled his way through a yellow notepad that was filled with tiny scribbled notes but found them impossible to decipher.

Something on the desk caught his eye. Peeking out from beneath a book on organic farming and another on coercive restraint therapy—

which sounded like either an oxymoron or something really, really unpleasant—was a thick printed document held together by binder clips. Arman slid it out and picked it up.

Typed on the title page were the words *Phase II*, and *Gary Powell III, MD* was listed as the author. Curious, Arman flipped to the next page. Then grimaced. Holy crap. The document was over *fifty pages long*. That didn't even include the table of contents. Knowing the limitations of his scant attention span, Arman proceeded to skim the thing, his eyes jumping from section to section.

> **Minimum requirements for participation in Containment must be met at all times. All members shall maintain their own Resource Levels, Emotional Harmony, as well as a Natural Physiological State. Failure to comply will be cause for Reabsorption.**

> **A Third phase, Integration, will follow shortly and will be outlined in a separate document. Please familiarize yourself with the distinctions between the Phases. Ignorance shall be no excuse for a lack of progression.**

> **Beneath Beauregard, the current leadership structure will be streamlined, with some positions eliminated altogether. This is necessary for maintaining Sterility. Should civil discord erupt, look to Sparta for guidance. Seek to destroy dissension. Else find a common enemy.**

> **Be warned! The immunosuppressant contamination of the more entrenched paths of Resistance will require elder-**

flower ointment for optimal healing. Apply liberally 3x/day.
May scar.

Arman set the Phase II document down. He didn't have the time or interest to get through the rest. What he'd read seemed far from helpful. Plus Beau was clearly accounted for in the Phase II plan. He gave one last look around. There was nothing else in the room—no more drawers to open or cabinets to rifle through—but Arman wasn't ready to give up.

Pushing open the office door as quietly as possible, he stuck his head into the hall. Used the flashlight to peer in every direction. There was nothing. No one. The coast was clear. After checking the lock to make sure he could get back inside, Arman held his breath, stepped into the corridor, and let the door shut behind him.

35

CREEPING DOWN THE HALL WITH as much stealth as he could, Arman tried every door he passed. None opened. He aimed the flashlight above him, and as he walked, he ticked off the words painted over the entryways. RESISTANCE. MORALITY. JUSTICE. MERCY.

Arman reached the staircase at the end of the corridor, on the far side of the building, and began to climb. Moonlight washed through the windows of the stairwell, guiding him up the steps and past the landing. Forget Dr. Gary's office, this was where he should've gone to begin with. It's where he'd seen the light last night and he suspected it was where Gary had brought Kira and all the other select community members. Kira had said the room was upstairs, and Arman was sure it was her he'd seen entering the building earlier—those sunlit braids. If there was evidence of collusion or blackmail or anything, it would be up here.

Wouldn't it?

When he got to the second floor, everything was grainy and still. An eerie grayscale space gaping like the mouth of a cave.

Arman took a cautious step forward, flashlight pointing ahead of him. There were only two rooms up here. Neither was locked. In fact the doors to both stood wide-open, begging for a choice. Arman squinted to read the words painted above each. The room to his left was ARDOR. On his right was KINDNESS.

It's important to me that your journey is paved with kindness.

Arman knew which room to choose, of course.

Beau had told him, after all.

He walked into Kindness bristling with rage. And certitude. This was the least he could do for Beau—follow the path toward truth. Refuse to give up.

He looked around eagerly, but also ignorantly—he didn't know what he was looking for. But as he scanned the space, Arman's rage faded into confusion. And despair.

There was nothing here.

Nothing. He stood in the middle of a conference room that was filled with plastic chairs and a couple of threadbare sofas. A folding table was set against the back wall, along with a couple of board games stacked on top of it and a few tattered romance novels. An empty water cooler and an ancient percolator both sat covered in dust. The whole place had the look and feel of an AA meeting where no one had bothered to show up.

Arman backed out of the room. It turned out there was nothing in Ardor, either. Just two chairs and an office phone and a pile of boxes filled with old pamphlets. Arman leaned to pick one of the pamphlets up. A dead spider fell out when he opened it. The date on the pamphlet was from five years prior, but it contained a basic outline of Beau's program and what he could offer. In the course descriptions section Arman learned there was a leadership track for people interested in fully committing to the Evolve lifestyle and supporting others in their journey toward Immunity. It cost three times the amount of the other courses. There was also mention of "investment opportunities," but no details were listed.

Arman scowled. This was clearly the room where Dr. Gary tried to get Kira to call her father. It had to be. In addition to the phone there was a musty-smelling mug with a moldy teabag pooling in it sitting on the windowsill.

Grabbing the phone, he sat in one of the chairs and scrolled through the digital call menu. The outgoing log contained ten calls. The first five were to random numbers. Probably relatives, Arman figured, and he wondered what the response had been. Arman's mom would no doubt burst into tears if he called asking for money. If she'd been drinking, that is. Otherwise she'd laugh long and hard. For good reason. She didn't have money. It's why she'd gotten remarried in the first place. Her new husband might be an asshole who hated the sight of her only son, but he was good for his share of the rent and so far had managed to keep his dumb ass out of jail.

Which was more than she could say about Arman's dad.

But the five most recent calls in the outgoing log were all to *Beau's* phone. Arman recognized the number. He'd programmed it into his own cell, on the day they'd first met and Beau insisted Arman could call him, day or night, with any questions he might have. Arman hadn't called—just knowing he could was enough. Only seeing that number now made no sense, because the time stamp on the calls were all within the last eight hours, which meant Dr. Gary had recently been in here, trying to reach Beau.

Over and over again.

On impulse, Arman hit the redial button and held the phone to his ear. He knew Beau wouldn't answer. That was impossible, right? The dead didn't stick around to keep their promises. But he wanted to hear Beau's voice.

He *had* to.

The phone rang.

And rang.

And rang.

maybemaybemaybe

On the eighth ring, Arman heard a click and a pause as the call switched over. This was promptly followed by a robotic female voice who came on the line to inform him that the mailbox he was calling was full.

He slammed the phone down.

Shit.

36

ARMAN LEFT THE RESEARCH BUILDING through the same window he'd come in. Only once outside he didn't turn back to the compound. He headed deeper into the forest, stumbling through the brush and following the moon westward. Toward the fern hollow. He didn't know where else to go.

He didn't know what else to do.

With nothing to show for the night's effort, Arman told himself he wasn't giving up on Beau and the search for truth. But there was too much he didn't understand. Too much he didn't know. Who was he to play amateur detective and go snooping around for a killer, anyway? He'd just screw everything up. Get himself killed.

But if the killer wasn't Dr. Gary, then who was it?

Well, Arman had no idea. That was the point. And given his general cluelessness, the best thing he could do, he decided, was to simply get the cook and leave this place. They'd go to the cops, who would know what to do. They could pull emails and phone records and bank statements, and find out who stood to gain the most from Beau's disappearance. Maybe Arman could even report the whole thing anonymously.

That way he and the cook could get on the road as soon as possible. Start a life together.

Without any burdens of the past.

Scrabbling down the steep ravine and into the dry creek bed, Arman kept the flashlight on to guide him. He wasn't worried about being seen. Not anymore. After all, it sounded like only Mari was looking for him, and she sure as hell wasn't going to make it out here in the dark. No way. He kept going. It wasn't long before he reached the bend in the creek. Saw the beds of soft ferns curling at his feet.

Using the light, Arman searched frantically for the flat rocks covered in pine needles. But he couldn't see them. Anywhere. Adrenaline pulsed through him. He set his bag down and searched more. Then gave a long sigh. There they were. Clearing the needles away, he crouched down and began to dig. He had to get the money now. It was imperative. Because he did *not* plan on coming back to this place once he'd left.

Ever.

The reality of his departure broke through as Arman dug deeper, loosing a guilty herd of what-ifs to thunder through his conscience.

What if I'd done the right thing when I first found him?

What if I'd really tried to get help?

Oh, Beau. I'm not forgetting you. I swear I'm not.

But it didn't matter, did it? Whether he forgot Beau or not was irrelevant. He'd failed. He hadn't found Beau's killer and that meant there was no foreseeable justice for the loss of someone so warm.

So wise.

Throat tight with sorrow, Arman felt his fingers touch plastic. Flashlight tucked beneath his chin, he reached into the hole he'd dug and carefully pulled out the bundle of bills. Sweet relief. The money was all there and all dry. Arman had just shoved the whole thing into his bag when a bright glint from the bottom of the hole caught his eye. He blinked. Leaned forward. There was something else in there. But that was impossible. He would've remembered if he'd put anything else in the ground and there certainly hadn't been anything in there before. Arman stretched his arm down and grabbed the object. It was heavy and cold. He thrust it beneath the flashlight's glow.

His skin crawled.

Wait. No. No. It can't be.

In Arman's hand was Beau's *knife*. There was no mistaking that polished blade—the whorled gleam of layered steel, forced together by brute strength and intelligent design. Only the knife's blade wasn't actually all that polished at the moment. Not anymore.

It was caked with dried blood.

37

YOU ONLY FEAR WHAT YOU *believe will kill you, never what will.*

Arman ran through the forest, sharp branches slapping his face, with Beau's heirloom knife still gripped tight in his hand. He didn't know where he was or where he was going.

All he knew was that his father had been right.

All this time.

The hows and whys of what Arman had done with the knife weren't all that important—an act of violence was an act of violence, no matter the reason—but he could still remember the white-hot rage he'd felt at learning Beau had told that market cashier he was a junkie. The way he'd stormed toward that van before blacking out.

Maybe that had been part of it. Hell, maybe that had been *all* of it. And every moment since, Arman had just been going in circles, chasing his own damn tail and skirting around things like logic and truth. Of *course,* he couldn't remember what had happened or burying the knife with the money—his brain was as cowardly as the rest of him, too chicken shit to face his own truth. And of *course,* he should've known. The clues were all there, right in front of him. No one else could've planned this. No one else could've known he would return to the compound and not go get actual help.

No one but him.

Arman ran faster. There was pain in each step and he relished it all. Maybe his own body was finally caving in on him, crumpling under the weight of his own weakness. His sins. God, he should've just swallowed those damn pills earlier. He wished he'd never found the knife. But then wishing for that was cowardly, too. This pain was pain he deserved.

He wound through the woods, his lungs burning, eyes still stinging, heading higher, until he rose above the clouds and the trees. Until the face of Echo Rock towered above him, more question mark tonight than exclamation point.

What are you going to do, Arman?

What now?

It wasn't hard to find the eastern trail that led to the peak. Arman started the climb. And unlike his first night here, he knew exactly what he was going to do when he got to the top. There was no doubt. No ambiguity. That path stood before him as bright and clear as the ocean on a sunlit day. It was all he could think of, that final leap. He didn't deserve a life with a beautiful girl.

Or with anyone.

The trail grew steeper. Arman's shoes slipped on the shifting earth and loose pine needles, throwing him off balance. Falling forward, he reached to grab onto the rocks above, trying to hold himself upright. In doing so, he was forced to drop the knife at his feet, and when he bent to retrieve it, Arman couldn't help but notice how easily it hid itself in the dirt and tree litter. A handy piece of camouflage. If not for the flashlight and the fact he knew the knife was there, Arman would never have been able to find it.

In fact, he realized, no one would.

Ten minutes later, Arman stood atop Echo Rock, with the wind rushing through his hair, huge whopping gusts that made the dark trees sway beneath him and the branches moan. If the truth was nothing more than proving a lie, then his proof—the knife—was now gone for good.

After giving a quick glance over his shoulder, Arman inhaled deeply and shut his eyes. Forced himself back to that first night here on this mountain, when he'd failed the one person who'd believed in him. He hadn't cut Beau that night because cutting Beau felt wrong. And Arman had wanted to be *right*.

But now, he just wanted to live.

Legs trembling, he cupped his hands on either side of his mouth and took a step forward.

"I'm so sorry," he cried into the wind. "Whatever happened, however it happened, and wherever you are, I never meant to hurt you! I never wanted that."

And then came the answer, flung back to him on the wings of the night wind, although not with a hundred voices, this time. Just one. It said:

"I'm so sorry. Whatever happened, however it happened, and wherever you are, I never meant to hurt you! I never wanted that."

AS IT SHOULD BE.

There's one last thing the girl wants you to know. One last thing she hasn't told you. At least, this is what she says when she calls in the middle of the night, after your invitation but before she fully commits.

You understand she's not having doubts in the true sense of the word. She knows what she needs, but knowing something and doing what it takes to get it are two fundamentally different processes. Knowing costs nothing.

Acting in one's own best interest can cost you everything.

So you listen to her worries with patience. With empathy, too. You're scared, you say to her in your soothing voice. You're leaving someone behind. This has to be it, because what else could it be? And that's when she tells you her story; the one about the boy with the cigarettes and the pretty mouth who broke her heart. Who left her for someone else. It's not a new story or a particularly poignant one, and it touches you only in its banality. In the fact that it's been told over and over and over again. There's a sadness in that.

It's tragic, really.

But confession breeds intimacy, which breeds devotion. After that the girl's yours. She's willing to follow wherever you go, and departure day arrives not long after. It's one of many for you. It's once in a lifetime for her. But you wouldn't have it any other way.

She meets you by the bank downtown, the big one. The Wells Fargo. You find her waiting in the parking lot not far from the ATMs. She hands you her bag and the final payment. She's good to go. She's more than ready.

When she's settled in the back of the van with the rest of the passengers, you hit the road. The girl's the last one you had to pick up and you like that. There's something to be said about the pleasure of anticipation.

There's something to be said about saving the best for last.

The trip down the coast takes hours, which is by design. Distance isn't always measured in miles or space. Sometimes it's a feeling. Or a change. Often, a chance. You arrive at the compound just as the day is coming to a close. It's a fond farewell. A sweet sip of good-bye for now.

The girl steps off the van and right then, you can see it in her eyes. You see it in the way the sun lights her hair and her smile warms your heart. First impressions are everything, and you know she's not going anywhere.

That's all you need. Just a moment. A promise. It won't matter what questions she's come here to ask. You already know she's found the answer.

And you love that.

That's the thing about seeking hope and clarity, freedom and well-being. None of us are immune to kindness or flattery or admiration. None of us can resist the sway of charisma. But there's power in helping others believe they can. In crafting truths that work to our advantage. After all, we're no different from the people we find. We have wants and hopes. And as there can be no truth without faith, there can be no us without them.

We all need other people to find ourselves.

And that, my friend, is as it should be.

38

ARMAN PEERED OVER THE EDGE of the cliff. Saw a single figure. A lit kerosene lantern.

"Beau?" he called.

"Arman," he said.

"You're okay?"

"I'm okay. How are you?"

"I'm confused right now. Really confused."

"I understand."

"You didn't try to kill yourself, did you?"

"No."

"And I didn't try to kill you?"

"Definitely not."

"But you wanted me to think that you did." The words spilled from his mouth before he had time to consider them. "You wanted me to think one of those things or both of them. Am I right?"

"Yes. I suppose. In a way."

Arman fingered his stitches. Felt the tenderness there. "Did you drug me?"

"Why don't you come down here? We'll talk."

So Arman walked back down to the clearing, where he and Beau sat on the ground facing each other, the lantern burning between them. Staring into the older man's affable, unlined face, those cool river eyes, Arman could almost believe no time had passed—that this was the same night when they'd sat together in the circle of watching eyes and Beau had held his hands.

Only it wasn't.

"I don't get why you'd do this," Arman said. "I don't get it at all."

"That's an understandable response."

"But this isn't an understandable situation."

"Then ask me. Ask me anything you want to know."

"Did you drug me? Is that why you told that guy at the store I was junkie?"

Beau nodded. "It's also how you hit your head. You fell. I'm sorry about that."

"But you knew where I was going to be that morning? That I was leaving?"

"I did."

"How?"

Beau lifted an eyebrow.

Arman's stomach dropped. "Wait. You mean—?"

"Yes."

Deep breath. He took a deep breath. "And who was the guy I talked to at Vespers? The one who looked like you? Who knew what you'd said?"

"That was my son, Paul."

"Your *son*?"

"That's right."

Arman's urge to dig at his wrist was stronger than ever. "And the Damascus knife. It's not one of a kind, is it?"

"More like a dime a dozen," Beau said. "But it's what you believed that mattered."

"I believed what you told me!"

"Most people do."

"And you somehow just knew I'd find the knife you'd buried? What if I hadn't gone back for the money?"

"You were always going back for the money, Arman. And when you found the knife, I knew you wouldn't kill yourself or turn yourself in. You'd do just what you did."

"Which was?"

Beau's eyes twinkled. "You found another way."

"So that was the plan? The whole point? For me to end up here?"

"That wasn't the plan. It was the conclusion. The ending. But if you think back on everything that's happened, everything you've done, you'll understand what the point was."

What he'd *done*? "All I did was screw things up! A lot of things. From the moment I got here."

"No," Beau corrected. "Don't tell me what you *think* you did. Tell me what happened."

"I . . . I felt good that you wanted me here. Then I felt terrible when I let you down."

"Not feelings, either. Events. Start from the beginning."

Arman blew air through his cheeks. "Fine. I got here. You asked me to keep a secret for you. Then I met a girl. She liked me. But I think you knew that."

Beau nodded.

"Then I didn't cut you with the knife. And when I thought you'd killed yourself, I didn't take you to a hospital. I came back here."

"Very good. What else?"

"I don't know. After that I was really confused. And scared. I thought

that Gary guy was trying to take over the camp from you. I told Mari
that." He paused. "Wait. Is *that* what you wanted me to do?"

Beau's lips twitched. "Hoped. I hoped you would."

"He's crazy, you know. Like, really crazy."

"I know."

"Yeah, well, other than that, all I did was convince my friends that
this place is evil. Then when I found the knife and figured I was the one
who'd hurt you, I . . ."

"You what?"

Arman felt sick. "I did something cowardly."

"Which was?"

"I buried it again. Somewhere else. I was going to just leave."

"But don't you see?" Beau said. "That was the point."

"It was?"

"Absolutely. What you did wasn't cowardly at all. You've learned
what you never could just by listening to me talk or trying to make me
proud. You've learned how to give a damn about yourself. How to do
what's necessary. Not what you think is right."

"You wanted me to learn that?"

"Of course."

"But *why*?"

"Well, that's a different question," Beau said. "And it's not just *my*
why. It never was."

"Then whose why is it?"

"You don't know?"

"No."

"Your father's."

Arman blinked. Very quickly. "What did you say?"

Beau leaned forward. "When I told you we were alike. I said that because I *knew*. Not just from what you'd told me. But because I truly know who you are. Where you come from and more important, who you could someday be. Those are the reasons I needed you here this summer. I told you that, too."

"So you know my dad? You actually know him?"

"In a way, yes."

"Jesus. That explains a lot."

"Does it?"

"I hate him."

"I know you do. Believe me."

Arman folded his arms. Licked his lips. "So you used me? Is that what you did?"

"Is that a bad thing?"

"I feel stupid."

"You don't have to."

"I could go to the cops. Tell them everything."

"I know."

"I might."

"That's your choice."

"But I don't *get* choices!" Arman cried. "That's the point. I never do."

"You will," Beau said.

They were silent for a moment.

"Is there anything else you want to know?" Beau asked finally.

He nodded. "Kira and Dale."

"I needed them to make you feel comfortable. But they don't know anything. That's the truth."

"Truth." Arman tested the word. It felt like heartbreak.

"Yes."

"One more thing."

"Okay."

"What's the doctrine of double effect?"

At this, Beau looked surprised. For the first time that night. "Where'd you hear that?"

"Some people were talking about it at dinner. It has to do with morality?"

"It does. It's a philosophical principle that states an immoral act can sometimes be considered moral if the greater good outweighs the smaller evil."

"And do you think that's true?" Arman asked.

Beau smiled his easiest smile. "Why, I don't think about it at all."

Later, when he was alone again, Arman dragged himself back down the mountain to the cook's cabin. He knocked on her window.

She opened it.

And smiled.

"Can I come in?" he said.

She nodded.

"Are you mad at me?"

"Why would I be mad?" she asked.

"Because I didn't find you earlier like I said I would."

"I know you didn't," she said.

Of course she did.

Arman crawled through the window. Not an easy task, given his state of exhaustion. She kept him from falling, then pulled him into her bed. Started to pull his clothes off. Hers, too. At first, he let her. At first he didn't care about anything else.

But then he stopped. Put his hand on hers.

"I want it to be different this time," he said. "Is that okay?"

"More than okay."

"I want to talk. I want to keep my eyes open."

"Me, too," she said.

So they did.

And after:

"Arman?"

"Yes?"

"Which would you rather believe in: a bad truth or a good lie?"

"The truth," he whispered. "Always the truth."

She touched his cheek. Kissed his brow. Reached beneath the sheets to run her fingers across the thick scars that lined his bare thighs.

Her hand lingered.

"What is it?" he asked.

"Do you remember what I told you the other morning? When I said that being part of a system that helps people change was the most important thing to me? That it was everything?"

"Of course. What about it?"

"That was all true."

He smiled. "But that's not bad."

"You're right," she said. "It's not."

39

WHEN HE WOKE THE NEXT morning, she was gone.

This didn't surprise Arman. It disappointed him, yes. But it wasn't surprising. Everyone had been using him. He realized that now.

He sat up in the bed in the empty room. The dust on the furniture made more sense in light of what he knew. This had always been a place of absence, and he was meant to leave, too. Arman dressed, gathered his things. Made his way outside into the early morning mist.

He walked down toward the iron gate with his head held high. He refused to hide or be fearful or take any route other than the obvious one. He didn't care who saw him and he didn't care what anyone else thought about his choices. Well, maybe he did care. A little bit. But less than he used to. So he would leave this place now, alone, and get a head start. In a few hours, Kira and Dale would leave, too. What happened after that was up to fate. Maybe the cops would come. Maybe there'd be a lawsuit. Maybe Beau would get arrested again.

Then again, maybe not.

"Arman!" a voice called out. "Wait!"

He held his breath before turning around.

It was Mari. Dear, dear Mari.

She was coming toward him along the path that led from the domed meeting hall. She was waving, too, in apparent excitement, although she didn't move very fast. Arman walked back to meet her, because that seemed like the kindest thing to do.

But he didn't know how to feel.

"Hey," he said.

"I've been looking for you," she told him. "Everywhere."

"Yeah, well, I'm leaving. You don't need to worry about me anymore. Although I didn't do anything. I didn't hurt Beau. Really."

"I know that," she said.

"You do?"

"That's what I wanted to tell you. I heard from him last night. Beau's fine, Arman. He's in San Francisco. I guess his van broke down on the way up north and he lost his phone. But he's there now. He says he might stay away for a while. He has traveling to do. But he's fine. He's absolutely fine."

"He is?"

She nodded, holding up her own phone. "Look."

Sure enough, there was a snapshot of Beau in San Francisco. God knew when it had actually been taken, but in the picture, he was smiling broadly, with Coit Tower in the background and the glittering bay beyond. Arman's throat tightened. He couldn't help thinking that if the photo were taken today, there'd be two people in it. Both smiling. Both celebrating being together again.

At last.

Arman looked away. Swallowed his anger. Or his grief.

Whatever it was.

"I'm glad he's okay," he said flatly.

"This is good news," Mari said. "Really good."

"I know."

"It means you don't have to leave."

"Oh, I think I should."

"But why?"

Arman couldn't tell her the real reason. So he forced a goofy smile on his face. The kind adults liked to see on him because it made him appear docile. "Look, I know I'm not going to be a part of Containment. I don't have the money. Or the status. So I might as well leave and save you the hassle of kicking me out."

Mari's eyes twinkled.

"Arman," she said. "Containment isn't happening."

"It's not?"

"No, it's not what Beau wants. It never was. We can't make the world a healthier place if we don't bring new people in. Teach them what we know. And while Beau's gone, I'm the one in charge. It's up to me to make sure we stay true to his vision. At all costs."

"But what about Gary? He said—"

"Don't worry about Gary."

"Yeah, but he's got plans to—"

"I know about his plans. And he's officially been relieved of his training position. As of last night."

"He has? Why?"

"It wasn't a good fit. The things he wanted to do, what he tried to make our visitors do, well, it wasn't in line with our purpose. It wasn't healthy. Just the opposite, really. I couldn't in good faith let him stay."

"So he's leaving?"

"He's already gone."

"Where'd he go?"

Mari paused. Then she placed a hand over her brow and gazed out over the hillside, her eyes focused on the horizon beyond. "Do you see all that, Arman? Do you really see?"

He tried following her line of vision. "See what?"

"Everything," she said. "Here we are, in the mountains, overlooking the sea. We're surrounded by miles and miles of forests and lakes and meadows and rocks and cliffs and waterfalls. Every kind of danger you can imagine. We're nothing here. Absolutely nothing. And that's a wondrous thing. To have so many places to lose ourselves in. To have so many ways to start over when the solutions we think we've found don't work."

A chill ran up Arman's spine, slick as a weasel, and he stared at Mari. He stared for a long time. At her sweet grandmotherly face. At that long, girlish braid and those soft, gauzy clothes, a fluttering reminder of power. There were so many questions he could've asked about what she'd just said.

But he didn't.

After a moment, Mari turned to smile at him. Gracious as always. "Beau also wanted you to know that you're welcome to stay here. For as long as you'd like. You've impressed him. He says you'd be a wonderful addition to the staff. That you have real leadership potential."

"Really? He said that?"

"He did. And I happen to agree."

"Well, thank you," Arman said, but he took a halting step backward. Felt the earth sway beneath him. "Can I, you know, think about it?"

"Take all the time you need."

Arman nodded and spun around. Started walking again. His legs felt weak and his heart fickle, but he had to keep moving. He had to get out of here. This place was crazy. Absolutely crazy. He couldn't stay and ignore all that, just because he was wanted.

Could he?

EVERYTHING.

Do you remember? Do you?

You sat in a coffee shop in Santa Barbara that day, at a table out on the covered patio. It was April. There was an ocean breeze and the scent of sea kelp in the air. The events of that summer were still vivid in your mind, but they were also far behind you. You'd made your choice and you were fine with it. There was no philosophy to life, you'd decided on that rich June day, before you'd called off Kira and Dale. Before you persuaded them to stay with you at the compound. Because they were your friends. True friends. It really was that simple. The same went for staying on your medication. There was no existential dilemma in that, no answers begging to be sought and no truths that would be better off just because you'd found them. Your needs were filled and the only truth you cared to follow was the here and now. That's what worked.

That's what mattered.

You'd been making plans that afternoon in the coffee shop—scoping locations, wanting to do everything just right. It was great being back in a college town. It wasn't your town, but what could be easier? You spied a newspaper resting on the next table over, discarded by a prior occupant, and you reached to grab it. It was the New York Times. *Sunday edition.* You read while drinking your soy latte, and you wished you'd asked for more foam. You often wished that, although asking for what you wanted had never come as easy as telling people what you needed them to hear. But you were working on it.

Evolving.

Your eyes skimmed the pages of the paper, suddenly catching on an article, or really, being caught. It was the profile of a man whose weeklong programs aimed at self-actualization and social resilience were becoming increasingly popular. There were training courses and sites popping up in different states. New York. Illinois. Oregon. California. Some people called it a cult. Or a con. But not the people who actually went. Those people used words like life-changing, transcendent, and most of all, healing. The courses were expensive, of course, but what price could you put on a lifetime of inner peace and empowerment, free from the bonds of emotional pollution and the chaos of disease?

There was a photograph, too, and you knew what you'd see even before you looked—the wise face of a fox who could always set his own snare when needed. That's what Beau was, wasn't he? Sly. Quick-witted.

In ways you couldn't help but admire.

You were right about what you'd see, of course. The picture of Beau was a handsome one. It was recent, too, taken near Lake George in upstate New York. He'd gotten sun, more color, but still there were no lines on his smiling face.

Not one.

What you didn't expect to see was the girl beside him, tucked under his arm with her cheek pressed against his chest. Your breath hitched not only because of their intimacy, but because even across newsprint and miles and countless lies, you still wanted her.

So very badly.

You read the photo's caption next. Your eyes danced past Beau's name to reach hers. Then you gasped. You couldn't help it. Because the truth wasn't the lie you expected; the cook you'd known with the bare legs and the yellow dress wasn't Beau's young lover. She never had been. She was his daughter.

Beatrice.

You smiled then, despite the wounding knife-twist of nostalgia, both because she was lovely and because there was still mystery in the world. You smiled, because in that moment—no matter the truth or the strength of the blade—you were something far more than nothing.

And that, you finally knew, was everything.